RIVER RUN

A CONSPIRACY OF RAVENS BOOK THREE

SHELBY LEE

table of contents

author's note

River Run is a dark, romantic suspense novel that contains triggering situations. It is a why choose novel, meaning our heroine does not ever have to choose between our three heroes. This book is intended for mature audiences 18+ and contains the word 'fuck' probably far too many times.

For a full content warning list, please visit:
http://www.authorshelbylee.com

raven

Drake looks at us apologetically as he puts gloves on. He moves to the other side of the table. "This, well, it might be jarring. Prepare yourselves."

I meet his gaze as I squeeze both River's and Phoenix's hands to the point of pain, then I nod.

Drake lifts the sheet, revealing the body.

When I muster the courage to look... all the air whooshes from my lungs.

"Alexis Sommers. Recently, let free of homicide charges. Again. Age 20. Daughter to Pastor Whitaker Sommers of Blue Lake, Oregon. Looks like a full drug overdose." He continues to speak, but I'm not listening anymore. A long breath leaves me, and I meet the gazes of Phoenix and River.

Lexi had caused us issues the last few months, but no one wanted her to die.

Not like this, anyway.

My phone burns a hole in my pocket. I need to text Pierce and find out where the hell he is.

"Just send the tox screen over to my private email, Drake, and I'll get it to a contact." Phoenix says. He meets my gaze, raises a brow, and cants his head to the side in question. When I shrug and turn toward the exit, he rattles off a few more instructions before saying goodbye and following us out.

"Anyone else kind of glad Lexi's gone?" River pipes up, and I chew the inside of my cheek, lost in my contradicting thoughts.

"Fuck, guys," Phoenix breathes, holding onto my hand for support. "I just wanted her to get help. Maybe she got the relief she needed. Death isn't always the worst fate."

I squeeze his fingers and rest my head on his shoulder as tears threaten to overflow.

Lexi may have tried to kill me, but did she deserve a death like this? Was she the bad one? Or was the world so bad she had to escape it somehow?

"So, that leaves the other thing," River says after we all climb back inside of the Jeep and he blasts the hot air again. "Where the fuck is Pierce?"

I keep my hands in my lap as I think. Pierce couldn't have left in the middle of the night. Not because he wanted out of this relationship. He couldn't have. He wouldn't have.

Not after the night we had.

Not after everything we've done.

"Let's just start back toward Junk. Maybe he's there? I've heard nothing from Lance or Agent Starling. That doesn't say much, though. They deal directly with Pierce most days." Phoenix sighs and starts up the engine, reaching over to grip my hand in one of his.

Halfway back, River's phone rings and his excitement is palpable.

"Holy fucking hell, you motherfucker. I might beat the absolute living shit out of you before I bend you over the couch and fuck you back into submission."

Phoenix coughs out a quick laugh and I glance at River with wide eyes and a throbbing heart.

The sinful visual of a dominant River does things to me, but now is not the time.

"I'm sorry, man." Pierce's voice comes out a little garbled through the speakerphone, but hearing it allows me to relax. "Agent Starling called me in to get some shit. They had me in an interrogation room for four fucking hours."

"Wait, why would more agents take you in if Starling is one? Isn't he the head of this team?" Phoenix's brows pinch together as he concentrates on both the road and what Pierce is saying.

"Yeah, he may have told me things I'm not comfortable talking about on the phone. When you guys get back to Junk, I'll explain everything." He clears his throat and I imagine him scratching the back of his neck like he always does when he's nervous. "I'll see you guys soon."

"See you soon," River says before cutting the line. He leans forward and presses a kiss onto my forehead, breaking away with a smile. "All's good in our little corner of the world, RaeRae."

I nod and rest my head against his temple, looking through the windshield to watch the snowflakes as they fall against the glass.

"LET her wake the fuck up before you just—" Phoenix's loud, gruff voice startles me awake, just before my door rips open and I'm pulled into a pair of strong and trembling arms.

Being woken up like this makes me shake. Being in Pierce's warm embrace after thinking he's been dead for most of the day is more fuel for my adrenaline. I barely have my eyes open before I slam them shut again, kissing him stupid and fisting the lapels of his leather jacket to pull myself closer to him.

He hums, his hands traveling to my ass as he holds me up, pressing my back against the Jeep, closing the door. The warmth of his body makes me forget how cold it is and that I don't have a coat on to begin with. "Fuck, Blue," he whispers against my lips. "Fuck, I'm so sorry for leaving like that." He kisses me again. "It was so stupid." Another kiss. "Forgive me." Kiss. "Please." He begs, kissing me once more after I nod.

"Pierce," Phoenix snaps, and Pierce groans as he pulls away. "She's not even wearing a coat, and it's fucking snowing. Let's get inside."

I roll my eyes, because the coddling of me needs to stop at some point. In an act of defiance, and because I feel like it, I lean forward to press my mouth to Pierce's again until we're both breathless, and I'm hot and bothered enough to fuck him right here in the middle of the snowstorm.

"He's right, little bird," Pierce whispers, pulling back. His lips glisten. They're swollen, still inviting, and when they kick up in his cocky grin, my heart skips a beat. "Let's get inside. River grabbed all the bags and I know he'll need help."

Sighing, I nod, wrapping my arms around Pierce's neck to hug him tight. A silent giggle leaves me when he carries me inside.

"If you didn't have her in your arms, PJ, I'd fuck you up right now." River grips Pierce by the jaw and slams their lips together in a display of dominance and gratitude that even I feel like a stalker watching.

When my gaze evades them, I see Phoenix studying us with his brows pinched and his arms folded over his chest. I pull my hands away from Pierce and sign, *Are you okay?*

I'm fine Red, he signs back, a soft, yet fake grin lifting the corner of his lips.

He turns to grab some bags and bring them upstairs.

"I'm sorry," Pierce says after River releases him. "Really, truly sorry."

"Tell us the whole fucking story," River snaps out after kissing my cheek. "Put her down so we can change. Then we'll sit down and talk this shit out."

Pierce places one last kiss to my lips and releases me, allowing my body to slide down all of his hard ridges until my feet land on the hardwood floor. Brushing a strand of hair from my face, he looks at me with worry shining in his eyes, and my heartbeat stutters to a near-stop.

Whatever happened is not as bad as death, but I'm worried it might be a close competition.

"SO," Phoenix says, a dark, ironic laugh leaving his lips, "let me get this straight. Agent Starling called you in the middle of the night. He said Jackson, come alone. And you just fucking went? Jesus, Pierce."

"Gotta say... it sounds dumb when you say it like that," Pierce grumbles, wrapping his arm around me once more, tugging me to his side.

As if I will protect him from being held accountable for leaving and making us worry.

Hell if he's getting that from me today.

I reach forward and grab my phone so I can text our group chat, making sure to *accidentally* land my elbow into his balls when I pull back and start typing.

"Fuck!" Pierce snaps out, glaring down at me.

I smile innocently and he narrows his eyes further.

"I need a fucking drink," River says, and Phoenix hands him a beer from the pack he'd already grabbed from the garage.

> Waking everyone up in the middle of the night would have been the best option, Pierce. We could have come up with a plan.

"Blue, that's—" Pierce tries to interrupt, but I glare up at him before continuing to type. He huffs out an annoyed breath, then grabs a beer for himself, popping it open with a hiss and drinking half of it before I'm done with my message.

> It doesn't matter what the issue is. We all need to work together. On everything. I'm sick of secrets, so you shouldn't have gone out on your own. You could have gotten extremely fucked up, Pierce. Maxwell. Jimmy. Now the FBI? This is ridiculous at this point. Never leave like that again. NONE of you.

I glance around the room when the message goes through, then let out a slow breath when Phoenix and River nod. Unfortunately, Pierce doesn't, and I glare at him until he does.

"Got it," he grits out. He chugs the rest of his drink before crushing the can and resting his head back on the couch. "Anything else anyone wants to yell at me for?"

"Your fucking attitude could use an adjustment," Phoenix says, smirking when River meets his eyes and nods in agreement. "Alright. What else happened, Pierce? Don't leave a damn thing out."

Pierce sighs and scrubs a hand down his face. He's so tired, having been up since the early hours of the morning, but Phoenix is right. He can't leave us out of anything. Not anymore.

"They shut down Alpha Mu last night during the Anti-Valentine's Day party; lots of fines given, arrests made. Maxwell is pissed. He hasn't stopped blowing up my phone because apparently Jimmy took off and is missing, too. He has no one to step up and run the frat."

"Wait, so Jimmy just ran like a little bitch?" River laughs, shaking his head.

"Yeah, but that worries me about what he might do to us. So we need to watch out for him in town and shit." Pierce stares down at me. That same worrying look from earlier crosses his features before he clears his throat and looks back at the other two. "I still have a few things to take care of when it comes to the frat. The feds kept me there. I was stuck in a boring ass room being asked questions about what the frat was a front for. I said we were all under duress, blackmailed, all that shit."

"What about Starling? Where was he?" Phoenix asks.

"That's the thing, I don't think he's a real fed." Pierce sighs and chews his lip in contemplation. "I think he's gone rogue, because he's been treating us like his own agents, his own team. We've done a lot of shit the feds know nothing about."

I peer around the room at the boys. How the hell did a bunch of young adults get into this shit in the first place? Sighing, I rest my head against Pierce's shoulder and breathe him in.

He wraps his arm tighter around me and rubs circles on my shoulder. "I think, in all honesty, we can trust him. We had a long conversation before I talked to the other feds. He told me what to say and what not to."

"You're trusting him too easily," Phoenix says, crushing his now empty beer can in his fist and tossing it into the trash as he walks into the kitchen.

"He seems to be the only one that gives a fuck about what's going on right now, Nix," Pierce snaps out.

"Okay," River says. "Slow down, boys. Don't fight over this. Not now."

"There's something else," Pierce says, his voice wavering.

Phoenix turns away from the fridge door, closing it as he leans back against it. Folding his arms, he raises a brow as he waits for this new threat.

"Mark Riley," Pierce says.

"What about him?" River asks, sitting up straighter in his recliner.

"We know where he is. I got information from my contact back home." Pierce blows out a breath and lets me go. He leans forward, his elbows on his knees, and clasps his hands together. "He's in Florida, and he's so off-grid, we can't call or even send a letter. Lives in a cozy little mansion with his daughter. They live on a property no one else steps foot on, trying to remain as inconspicuous as possible."

"Are you ever going to tell us who this contact is?" Phoenix asks. "Quite frankly, Jackson, I'm over being in the dark on things. Even Lance and Agent Starling talk to you more than he does to us."

"Agreed," River says.

I nod in agreement, keeping my eyes locked on Pierce's so he knows I mean it. He won't keep anything from me again.

Sighing, Pierce runs a hand across his tired face. "I swore I wouldn't say a damn thing about who he is. He has a vested interest in things, and he hardly tells me anything, either. It's not like we're best friends."

"Whatever," Phoenix bites out, turning around to grab an apple from the fridge. He takes a bite, walks back into the living room, and sits down on the other end of the couch.

"It's not that I'm intentionally keeping secrets, Nix. You know that." Pierce looks at him over my shoulder, and the tension between them threatens to suffocate me.

"You hide too much shit, Jackson. Too much." Phoenix glances out of the window, dismissing the chance for more conversation.

So what do we do about him being in Florida?

"We gotta go find him. He's the only one who might know more. He might be able to stop Maxwell for good." Pierce stands up and walks to stand next to Phoenix. The sun is setting, and the eerie glow of red around him makes my gut churn. "If nothing else, we can have him make an anti-drug for at least us four."

"Or," Phoenix chimes in, "he could teach me how to make it and I can teach others. We can save this campus. We don't have to be the only ones who get the benefit of living."

"Yeah, well," Pierce sighs. "I only care about the four of us right now."

"What else was said?" River asks.

"What do you mean?" Pierce turns to look at him over his shoulder. "I said everything."

"No, you haven't," River snaps. "There's something else, Pierce. What are you hiding?"

"Nothing!" Pierce shouts.

I jump and he winces.

"Secrets, Jackson. They'll get us all killed." Phoenix pulls me into his side and I sigh, closing my eyes. I don't want to see the frustration in any of their gazes right now.

No one speaks for a few minutes. It's uncomfortable. The intensity rises in the room again as the tension begins to boil over.

"Human trafficking," Pierce says so softly I almost miss it.

"What?" River asks, voice unsteady like he heard Pierce, but doesn't want to believe it.

"They're dabbling in human trafficking." Pierce grimaces. "It's bigger than just Maxwell and CU, too."

"By dabbling, do you mean just starting or...?" Phoenix asks. He's squeezing his apple so hard the juice is coating his arm.

"They've been trafficking the girlfriends of Alpha Mu guys for... a long time," Pierce says. "It's infuriating. They had pictures of all the girls, plus others, in Maxwell's desk."

"Wait," River says. "That was why those pictures were there? Those were victims? Targets?" His panicked eyes flit toward me, then back to Pierce, his own growing wide. "But—"

"Yeah. They were current targets."

I must be missing something here. The way both of them are looking at me, and how Phoenix's body tenses...

Shooting to my feet, I rush toward Pierce, shoving him hard enough that his body slams into the glass and his head smacks into it. Before I can think to stop it, I whip my hand out and slap him, leaving behind a handprint. Too furious to sign what I want to say, and even more infuriated I can't yell at him. I ball my hands into fists. Phoenix lifts me by the waist and pulls me several feet back, saving Pierce from being pummeled into the ground.

River rushes to Pierce's side and holds his head in his hands, examining the red shaped mark of my handprint on his cheek. A small smirk plays on his lips when he looks back at me, but when he sees the fury aimed at him, too, he frowns. "Shit," he mutters. "Rae, we didn't want you to worry about this."

"Wait," Phoenix says, setting me down but keeping me under his arm. "You knew about this too, River? You fucking knew?"

River holds his hands up and shoots me an apologetic glance. "When we went to Maxwell's office, photos of Rae were in there. A series of photos. Mixed in with other girls." He audibly swallows when he looks at me. "RaeRae. I really am sorry. Honestly. I—" He pleads with me, but fuck that.

I hold my hand up to stop him. After an achingly long silence, I flip him off and turn on my heel, shoving past Phoenix and heading upstairs to hide in the blankets and get lost in a book featuring a group of vampires, a girl who sometimes dies, and a ghost.

Fuck these boys.

It'll be a hard won battle for them to turn into real men.

river

"I swear you guys are some of the biggest idiots ever and you're lucky she fucking loves you. I'm tempted to take her away, but unlike you two, I know how *not* to piss her the fuck off." Phoenix sighs and tosses his apple in the trash before following Rae up the stairs.

Can't blame him for being her white knight when her other two are the dark horses who only hurt her over and over again.

"Fuck," Pierce says as he rubs at his cheek. "I sometimes regret teaching her how to hit like that."

I scoff, then let out a laugh. "You taught her how to bitch slap?" I narrow my eyes on the mark and wince when I see a small drop of blood where her nails punctured his skin.

"I taught her a lot. Wish I would have listened and learned from her, though." He sighs and rests his head against the window as we both find a comfortable sitting position, allowing the glass to cool us down.

"I don't know how to deal with all of this, Pierce. My dad's involved with Maxwell, and I know he was... not doing good things to those kids." I bring my knees up and wrap my arms around them.

"You *were* one of those kids, Riv. It's okay for this to fuck with you, and it's absolutely okay to be pissed." Pierce wraps his arm around me and tugs at me until my head rests on his shoulder.

"They're after Rae. We have to watch her like a hawk now."

"We already are," Pierce says. "But listen, this goes deeper. Lexi's father is involved, too."

"So what?" I bark out a sharp laugh. "It's just *let's go to church and get sold* and no one is saying a damn thing?"

"You," Pierce says. "You can say things."

"I'm not ratting out my father. He'll hurt my mom, man." I shove away from him, only to get pulled back in.

Pierce grips the back of my head in his hand and slams our foreheads together, glaring right into my eyes. "River, listen to me. Your secrets are your secrets, but they could also be someone's fucking freedom."

I shake my head, tears threatening. "Let go of me. Now," I spit out.

"You're being a pussy," he tells me and I reach up to grip his jaw between my fingers.

Two of us cannot dominate in this situation, and I refuse to let him come out on top.

Not anymore.

Not since Rae.

"You're walking on thin fucking ice, Jackson."

He jerks back as if I've hit him, but I keep my hold on him. He glares harder and clamps his teeth together.

"I will not rat my father out unless I have a million and one protections in place. One of those being the rest of this house's safety. Another being my mother's ability to get clean after all these years." I release his jaw and stand up, slamming my hand on his shoulder when he tries to stand. "I should make all of your darkest fucking nightmares come true, because that's the shit that happened when you didn't answer your damn phone."

"Riv, I—"

"Shut the fuck up!" I bellow, and footsteps sound before Raven's sweet face appears around the corner. I meet her panicked gaze and throw my hands out to my sides. "Is this what everyone fucking wanted? To see me explode into a trillion pieces?"

"Riv—" Pierce tries to stand, but I glare at him hard enough he flinches.

"I may be fucking cool and collected a lot of the time, but for the love of everything," I growl and my hands twitch to grab something. To hurt something. To take all of this anger out on the world and destroy the things that mean the most to me.

It's what I've always done. What I've always known.

Rae walks up to me, brows pulled together and a frown on her lips. Phoenix tries to catch her arm once he sees the situation, but she holds a hand up to stop him.

My skin vibrates with the anger running through my system, and I clench and unclench my fists half a dozen times by the time she makes it to me.

Talk to me, she signs.

I shake my head. My brain rattling in my skull as I attempt to draw deep breaths to abate the destruction I crave to cause. She can't be part of it. "Rae," I plead with her. It's barely more than a whisper. "Please, back away."

Pain crosses through her eyes and I want to take it back, but I also know it's what's best.

"Nix," I growl.

Phoenix nods and walks up to Raven, grabbing her hand and pulling her back toward the stairs with him. They both look over their shoulders at me in concern before disappearing.

"River," Pierce says from his spot on the ground.

I hold up a finger, take another deep breath, then turn toward him with the fire of a thousand suns blazing from my eyes. "Up on your knees, pup."

"This isn't the time to get your dick sucked, man. We need to talk this out before you—"

"The only way I'm going to explode right now is down your throat." I snap my fingers and take sick satisfaction at how quickly he does as he's told. Pavlov had something right, that's for sure.

Pierce's gaze burns into me, but I don't meet it, even as he seeks mine out from his new spot on his knees.

"Take my cock out, and put it in your mouth," I demand.

Coming to terms with what he is about to do, he blows out a long breath and fumbles with the button on my jeans before pulling down my pants and boxers, freeing my half-hard dick to the cool air surrounding us. "This will fix nothing."

"I don't care what it fixes." When his hand connects with my shaft, I groan, tossing my head back. "I just want to use this energy elsewhere. Where better for it to go than directly to my dick?"

"You're an idiot," Pierce mutters, yelling out when I clutch his hair in a tight vise.

"What was that?" I hiss, glaring down at him. "I

shouldn't hear a fucking word from you, Pierce. Your mouth should be all over my dick, not running away from you with bratty fucking comments."

He splutters another argument, or maybe it's an apology, but I grip his jaw and spit into his mouth, groaning as I watch it slide to the back of his throat. I grasp myself with my empty hand and place the tip against his parted lips. "Suck me off like a good boy and I might not kill you for making us believe you were dead for half the day."

He starts to talk again, but I don't let him get a single word out. I shove so far down his throat that tears spring free and his glare threatens to burn a hole through the universe. My lips twist into a wicked smile as I hold there, my grip on his hair tightening further when he gags and tries to tear away.

"We seriously thought you were gone, you motherfucker." I swallow the lump in my throat and pull back when his face reddens.

He gasps for air and grips my thighs in his hands, his fingers digging in.

Like a good boy, he says nothing, leaving his mouth wide and tongue out for me to shove back in.

I do.

Fuck, I do.

"I swear I know Heaven only exists because your mouth and Raven's pussy are the closest I've ever gotten to it." I groan when he traces his tongue around my tip, and bite down on my lip hard when he reaches with one hand to tug at my balls. "Ah shit."

He bobs along my shaft, tracing the length of me and pulling me to the back of his throat. He swallows, and my knees buckle at the added pressure.

I grip his head with both of my hands and start face fucking him like I always dream of doing. We may have started this before Rae, but he's only allowed me to have more control since she's been here. It's like he can finally be himself now that we're all under the same roof.

Smirking, I dart my eyes up to the loft, knowing she could watch if she really wanted to.

I meet her gaze and wink when I catch her beautiful thighs shifting, seeking the friction she could so easily get with Phoenix.

She keeps watching us though, so I go back to thrusting into Pierce's mouth to give her the show of a lifetime.

Pierce sucks me like the filthy cocksucker I've trained him to be, and the sight is enough to send me far beyond Heaven within seconds.

A shame, because I'd planned to make him sore as fuck so he couldn't use his words to harm people for at least the next few hours.

"Fuck," I groan as he continues to suck me down, running his hand along my shaft as I come down his throat. "Oh, fuck."

He pulls back and gasps for air. When he starts to swallow, I grip his jaw in my hand and shake my head, tilting him so he can look up and see our audience.

"Show her how well you swallow my cum, pup. Show her how much you like the taste of me as it slides down your throat." I collar his neck and grin when he does as he's asked, my dick nearly coming back to life at the overwhelming sense of power I feel when I dominate him. "Good boy," I whisper.

Pierce keeps his gaze on Raven for a few beats, but looks back at me when her footsteps fade into the distance. His eyes are hungry, but I'm about to make him a very pissed off pet.

"Go clean up, then meet me in the garage," I tell him, kissing his temple before pulling my clothes back on.

"The fuck?" he asks incredulously.

"Learn another lesson, Pierce. Your actions have consequences now." I sing-song the last bit as I walk out, throwing my hand up in a wave.

Of course, getting off doesn't shoot away the nasty memories of my past, so I grab a beer, sit my ass on a stool, and let them have me as I wait for Pierce to do as he's told.

"RIVER," *my father says as he enters the church hall. He has a smile on his face, a bag of chili cheese fries in one hand and a coke in the other.*

"Father," I say in response, our normal greeting. I accept the offered drink and bag of fries, digging my hand inside and grabbing the container. I dig in, not caring how messy my hands are about to get.

At least it's with chili and cheese, and not other things.

"You did good this past month. Got a whole ten kids to come to the youth group." He sits down next to me and slaps me on the back.

I choke on one of my fries, quickly taking a drink to wash it down. Nodding, I look out over the rows upon rows of chairs in my father's church, the red fabric and carpet even more ominous now that I know exactly what he uses his notoriety for.

"You could have done better though, son." He makes this

noise in the back of his throat that clues me into his anger. "I expect twenty next time."

"Funny," I grit out, taking another handful of fries and stuffing them in my mouth. This food is short-lived, and I'm hoping to eat most of it before—

He grabs the container and shoves it into the bag, glaring down at me. "If you think that's funny, I'm sure you'd love to see the end of my belt again, too."

I wince and shake my head as I lick the mess from my fingers. "No, thanks."

He holds his hand up to his ear and leans uncomfortably close to me. "What's that?"

I clear my throat and sit up straighter. "No thank you, Sir."

The words are like sandpaper on my tongue, but I say them anyway.

He grins this wicked grin and pats me on the leg, glaring daggers when I flinch at his touch.

Guess why, asshole.

He holds me down in my spot when I move to stand.

"I expect the best behavior this Sunday, son. I don't care what you have to do to keep more of the young adults coming. Just keep doing it."

I hate this. I hate it so much. I've been bringing kids in for years now. Like a little pawn. His little bitch.

Unfortunately, it took me too long to realize some of them were going missing shortly after joining our youth group, and when I realized it, I went on a bender for three days and ended up in the hospital where they had to pump my stomach so I didn't fucking die.

I still bring people to the church, though.

Robert Jacobs has me by the balls, sometimes literally, and is holding my mother's life over my head like a carrot in front of a horse.

"I'll give you that motorcycle you want if you think it'll help. Maybe go traipse around Valley. Bring some of those heathens here. God will save them." He stands up and pats me on the shoulder again before tossing my half-eaten fries into the trash. "Your night to do the opening prayer, River. Make it a good one. Scare them a little, too, yeah?"

I nod and sip from my coke, my eyes locked on his feet as he leaves the sea of red behind him.

"RIV?"

I startle, and my eyes narrow in irritation. "What?" I snap, glaring at Pierce, though he only looks concerned.

"I've been calling your name for ages, man. What's running through your head?"

"My father. Other shit. I'm keyed up." I stand up and shove past him as I make my way to the toolbox in the corner of the garage. "Let's do a full tune-up of the Jeep. If we're going to Florida, we'll be on the road for a while."

Pierce watches me with a worried expression, but grabs a jack and walks over to the Jeep. "Guess we're going on a fuckin' road trip."

RIVER

Hey, sweet girl…

raised brow emoji

RIVER

Listen… I know you're locked up like a
princess in a tower. It's stupid. I'm really
pissed at Pierce right now.

YOU'RE pissed at Pierce?

RIVER

Fuck yeah, I am! He's doing stupid shit.

But you following in his fucking footsteps
ISN'T doing stupid shit?

RIVER

Fair point…

But uh, can I at least tell you how sorry I
am for how he's treating you?

No, River, you can't apologize for him. That
fixes nothing. Go back to being a good dog
and leave me alone.

RIVER

Okay…

I don't do everything he tells me to, you
know?

Raven?

You're ignoring me now? I didn't do
anything wrong!

But if I did… I'm sorry.

raven

I stare at the question on my screen for longer than I'd ever like to admit.

How the fuck am I supposed to have the answer to that?

Selecting C, because that's what the last three were, I submit the quiz to my online course and slam the laptop shut. I huff and lean back against Phoenix, closing my eyes.

I'm so tired.

He chuckles and bands an arm around my chest, pulling me into him. "Done, Red?" he asks. His breath is hot against my skin and I shiver.

I nod and grip his forearm with both of my hands, holding him as closely as I can manage.

He puts the book he's reading down onto the nightstand and uses his free hand to tilt my head to the side. Smiling, he leans in and kisses me with a raging intensity.

"Hell," he says. His smile is charming and warm as he pulls away, and both of us are breathless.

I grin and shrug, eyes heavy lidded and distorting my view.

"Tempting as you are," he draws out, nipping at the end of my nose. "I have a phone call to make." He slides out from the bed.

I stick my lower lip out in a pout, fold my arms over my chest and stare at him, watching as he adjusts his dick in his pants. Raising a brow, I shift my gaze back to meet his.

He's not even looking at me. Instead, his phone is in his hand and he's glaring at it, furiously typing out a response to something. Without even a last glance in my direction, he storms off down the stairs. When the back door opens and shuts loudly, I sigh.

I have no idea how to fix his frustrations, but I realize it has everything to do with the death of Alexis Sommers. If he was that in love with her, why did he leave her?

I still feel like I'm out in the cold when it comes to his story.

Standing from the bed, I stuff my hands inside my hoodie pocket and walk to the railing, looking down into the loft. Not a single other soul around.

Where the living fuck is everyone?

I turn and study the bedroom. When the clang of something being tossed rings out, I jolt, rushing down the stairs with my pulse pounding in my throat.

"Motherfucker!" River shouts as I enter the garage. He tosses a tool at the toolbox against the wall. "Dumb fu–Oh!" he says, eyes widening when he sees me. "Hey, RaeRae."

As if he's been waiting for me, he takes a deep breath, then clenches and unclenches his fists a few times as he brings them down to his sides. He cocks his head to the side, grins, and stuffs one hand into his pocket. He's so full of shit.

What's got you keyed up? I sign.

"Dunno what you're talking about, Rae." He turns around and leans down to study the front passenger side. "Hey." He looks back at me. "Know how to change a tire?"

I sigh and shake my head as I step over a few tools which are tossed on the cold garage floor.

Thank fuck for the fuzzy sock collection the guys keep building for me.

"Alright." River hands over a shiny stick with what looks like a thermometer on it. "You need to stick this over the valve stem. It'll check the pressure for you. The Jeep needs to be between 32 and 36 PSI."

I do as he tells me to, and watch as the meter fluctuates until it reads 29 PSI. I don't know what to do, so I wait for the next instructions.

"Now you take the air hose," he hands a small hose to me. "Place it over the valve stem, and I'll turn it on. You'll have to keep checking to make sure it doesn't get too much air, but I'd say put it at about 34 and we'll call it good."

I place the end of the hose over the valve stem and wait for him to turn on the air. Once he does, I wait and watch until it gets to 35 PSI.

"Good!" River says over the noise. He turns it off and comes over to my side, recapping the tire. "Next thing you know, you'll be looking at a tire and just *knowing* it's in the right range." He leans over and kisses my temple.

Will you tell me what was wrong? I sign, catching him off guard.

He winces and stands up, reaching out for me. He pulls me up by the hands and kisses my forehead.

"Alright, let me teach you how to change the oil. I gotta do something else while discussing all of my downfalls, RaeRae."

I roll my eyes and kiss his throat before pulling back and nodding.

"Alright," River says as he walks over to the open hood. He leans over it and I watch as his muscles flex beneath his white shirt.

Fuck, these boys are sinful.

"Did you hear me?"

I snap my gaze up to meet his and shrug.

He chuckles and shakes his head. "Stop ogling me. I'm trying to be a gentleman and ignore how you look like sex on legs in my hoodie."

I glance down at myself. Guess this is his. I shrug and bite my lip to hold back my grin.

"Come over here. I'll show you how to change the oil."

I walk over to him and he pulls me under his arm, tucking me between his chest and the hood.

He spends the next few minutes explaining how to check the oil and how to change it. He walks me through every step he takes, then sighs when the oil is draining into a pan. His clothes wrinkle as he slides from under the Jeep, and when he stares up at me, he pulls his lower lip between his teeth and chews on it for a second. "Guess I owe you an explanation, huh?"

I plop down next to him and cross my legs, nodding my head.

"When I was a young kid, I used to love to go to church with my dad. We'd get there early, help set up, then leave after everyone else. Just the two of us." River sighs and scrubs a hand down his face.

I grin when I see the streak of grease that leaves behind. Handing him a rag, I wave for him to continue.

"Thanks." He wipes the stain from his skin before gazing up at the ceiling. "After a few years, my dad started doing a lot of shit he probably shouldn't. It was fucked, Rae." His eyes shift to meet mine and my heart clenches at the pain I see in them.

I'm sorry, I sign.

"Not your fault." He shakes his head and blows out a breath. "So, eventually, I tried to tell my mom." He laughs. "Yeah, that didn't work so well. Dad beat me for," he puts his hands up in air quotes, "*disturbing my mother's peace*. Like I was the one who caused the entire issue to begin with. Stupid as hell if you ask me." He shifts his gaze up at the ceiling again and winces. "That's when I found out she was on drugs. Had been for a long time. She's been high my whole life. When I think back, there isn't a single moment she wasn't out of it. Makes sense now that I know they're friends with Maxwell, huh?"

I shrug and chew on my thumbnail, my mind wandering. What would my life be like if my mom hadn't taken me? Or aunt. Whoever she was to me, she was my mother. She raised me.

She was everything.

I swipe aside a tear and grab for a nearby wrench, twirling it in my hands as I watch River.

He tinkers with something to keep himself busy. "When I told him I was going to college, he was mad at me. I was supposed to be a minister and be a youth preacher. All that shit." He shrugs. "I came to CU to get away from it all." Gray eyes shift to meet my gaze again. "He went from calling me twice a day, then to once a week to tell me I've made a dumb mistake. He's picked up since New Year's Eve, but I refuse to answer him at this point. I have too much good going for me now to worry about his bullshit."

Does he expect you to come back after college? I sign, hands shaking at the thought of *after*.

"Absolutely." He sighs, and my heart clenches. "I won't, though. I don't know where I'm going after college." He looks down at the oil pan and switches it out before standing up and leaning against the hood of the Jeep.

I peer up at him with an ache in my chest, then sigh and stand next to him.

He wraps an arm around my shoulders and pulls me close, resting his cheek on top of my skull. "Pierce and I—"

"We what, Riv?" Pierce snaps as he enters the garage with a few bottles of water and a bag of chips. "Gonna talk for me now?"

"No," River grits out, snagging a bottle out of Pierce's hands.

"What are you doing out here without shoes on, little bird?" Pierce hands me a bottle as he steps closer to me.

I shrug and point to my warm fuzzy socks as I take a sip.

"Fair enough," he says. He grins as he looks over at River. "Showing our girl how to take care of a car, huh?"

"Apparently you never did," River retorts.

"She never would stand still long enough to listen." Pierce glances back at me and as his eyes rake over me, my body heats.

Damn these men.

"Rae," Pierce whispers, reaching out for me. He pauses. "Can I touch you?"

I bite my lip, giving enough of a dramatic pause for him to take a step back, then nod.

Frustration seeps into his features, but he leans forward and places a gentle hand on my cheek. He leans in and kisses me. Full of the love and passion he seems to save for me, and only me.

My heart skips enough beats that I worry for my health, but he pulls back and places his forehead against mine, our noses resting against each other's.

"I love you," he whispers.

I nod, wishing I could say it out loud.

"You two look so good together," River muses. He leans against the hood next to me and reaches forward, stroking his hand through my hair.

Pierce grins as he pulls back, grabbing the rag from River's pocket and wiping it down my cheek. "You had a little grease stain there, Blue. You getting a little dirty in here?"

I smile and shrug, eyes darting to meet River's gaze.

He winks at me. "Yeah. A little dirty. You interrupted, of course."

"Of course." Pierce leans down and kisses the side of my neck. "Let me apologize to you?"

I toss my head back, allowing him more access to the skin there. Water sloshes onto our feet when I drop the bottle in favor of sliding my fingers through Pierce's black hair, tugging when he bites my skin.

"You gonna apologize to her or her pussy, pup?" River asks, leaning in to kiss the other side of my neck.

Overwhelmed by the sensations coursing through my body, I don't care what they apologize to so long as they leave me satisfied at the end. I'm too worked up.

Pierce groans in my ear, and I squeeze my thighs

together in search of friction. Any friction. "You taste like heaven and hell all combined."

"Look like it, too," River adds.

My legs wrap around Pierce's waist when he lifts me, and our lips meet in a dirty kiss. My nails score down his scalp and neck. Tug at his shirt. Tear at his skin in an effort to get closer.

"Shit, Rae," Pierce grunts. "Hold on." He sets me on a tool bench, and rips my pants and underwear down, discarding them and my wet socks. He falls to his knees and my pussy grows wetter.

These men at their mercy before me are my favorite treat.

River comes over and slides my shirt and hoodie off of me, tossing it to the ground behind him. He leans in and places those sinful lips of his over one of my nipples and my hips buck forward.

Pierce grabs both of my thighs and holds them tightly in his hands, squeezing when I twitch. "You wanna come for us, little bird?"

I nod frantically and they both chuckle.

Dickheads.

I reach down and grip Pierce's hair, tugging his face closer to me until his nose brushes over my clit. Just enough to spark more of a fire low in my belly. I wrap my other hand in River's hair, pulling until he moves away from my breast and kisses me.

He reaches out and plays with my nipples, alternating between each side until I'm squirming against Pierce's face.

Pierce thrusts his tongue inside of me and I shoot off the table, only to be held down with his hands. He scratches his nails down my thighs, and the mix of pain and pleasure builds an orgasm so strong that one more flick of River's finger over my nipple makes me detonate around him.

My body seizes as I climax, clutching onto both of them as I kiss River and Pierce continues to stroke inside of me. They both ride it out with me until I'm just a tired, sated mess on the workbench.

"Filthy girl," Pierce says as he pulls away from me, wiping his mouth off with his hand.

River leans down and grasps Pierce's jaw. "Share like a good pup." He then kisses Pierce as if his life depends on it, groaning when Pierce grips River's bicep to keep himself steady on his knees.

I watch them greedily until I'm sure I could come again if they looked in my direction.

River pulls away and rises, adjusting himself in his pants. "We have to tell her more of our secrets, Pierce. I'm tired of her being in the dark."

Pierce sits back on his haunches and looks up at me. His eyes darken, and his nostrils flare as he takes a deep breath and lets it out. "Okay," he says as he stands.

River hands me the hoodie and my underwear, helping me into both of them like a child.

I snatch the clothes and put them on, raising a brow at him.

They act like I can't fucking handle my shit.

Pierce holds his hand out, intertwining our fingers together when I place mine in his. He tugs me to the Jeep where River slid under the hood. We pause and watch when he takes off the white shirt, tossing it to the ground.

"Greedy, greedy, little vixen," River says, winking up at me when our gazes collide.

I shrug and sit down next to him. I shift my gaze to Pierce, waiting impatiently for the answers he owes me.

"Alright, well." He sighs, leaning his head against the large toolbox, making it rattle.

"Get on with it, pup," River bites out, sliding back under the hood.

"Maxwell has been heading up some human trafficking efforts." Pierce winces. "And it looks like he's been working alongside River's dad and Whitaker Sommers as well."

Alexis' dad? I sign, eyes widening in shock.

"The only one surprised about that particular fact is you, Rae," River says.

Pierce clears his throat and slides his thumb along my palm as he meets my gaze. "There were pictures of you inside his desk and Jimmy's room. We told you that part. There were plans for you. Jimmy paid for you."

I flinch backward and press my hand to my chest to try to stop the erratic beating of my heart.

"We won't let that happen. Never. Not you. You aren't his. You're—"

"Ours," River finishes for him as he slides out from under the hood. He sits up and kisses me long enough that I become breathless for an entirely different reason. "You got that, little vixen? You're ours and we're yours. We'll never let them take you."

I breathe him in until my heart rate steadies, then nod.

"Good. Now, as for Mark Riley?" River asks, looking at Pierce.

"We're gonna go find him. All this work on the Jeep is to make it road trip ready." Pierce looks down at our hands, then back until his eyes meet River's. "Hopefully, he'll help us get an anti-drug out there so we can distribute it. I don't want people dying like this."

"Me either," River supplies before sliding back under the hood. "Spring break starts next weekend, so it won't even look like we're running."

I chew on my lip as I think about taking a road trip to interrogate some old guy who hasn't interacted with anyone from this side of the country for nearly two decades.

"I know this sucks, and it's terrifying, Blue," Pierce says, meeting my gaze again. "We'll have Lance and his guys to watch over us, however they need to. Maxwell will be back here, or wherever he goes, for spring break. Jimmy was talking about going to the Bahamas." Pierce grins and my lips tilt up to mimic the gesture. "Who says this has to be for a purpose, anyway? We can enjoy ourselves, too."

What's even on the way? I sign.

"Vegas. New Mexico. New Orleans." Pierce's smile widens at the last one. "You've always wanted to go to New Orleans, right, little bird? Now you can go."

I nod and smile brightly, letting myself pretend for just a little while that we're all normal college kids, about to embark on a happy and exciting adventure for spring break.

A girl can dream, right?

CHAPTER FOUR

I pace around the room, packing up the last little things everyone keeps forgetting to grab.

Chapstick.

Pillows.

Chargers.

It's like they all decided we didn't need a damn thing on this trip aside from ourselves. And the sex toys. River grabbed those and labeled them a priority, so that box is the final one to be packed.

I place my head in my hands while sitting on the end of the bed.

The stress of this entire situation is going to break me apart piece by piece.

Add in Lexi dying, not a single person contacting me about a funeral, and the fact I'm even remotely considering someone killed her... I'm a volcano about to erupt.

My phone rings, and I snatch it out of my pocket, answering it before I can check the name. "Hello?"

"Hey, Nix."

"Ryan?" I ask, standing as if I could go to him. "What's up?"

"Been a while," he says, letting out a light laugh.

"Yeah, man, it has." I peek over the railing and watch River grab Rae around the waist, tugging her to him before tickling her mercilessly. "It really has."

"Listen," Ryan sighs. "I have news for you. Not sure how you'll take it, but I still wanted you to know."

I clench my jaw and take a deep breath. "What's going on, Ry?"

"Lexi's dead, man." His voice hitches, and he clears his throat.

While everyone hated her, more for what she'd done than anything else, we all still fell under her spell at one point. Unfortunately, the world fucked her over more than she fucked it over.

"Shit," I whisper. The only reaction I feel I can have without cluing him in that I already knew.

"Yeah."

A beat passes before he sighs again, and I listen as someone cries in the background.

"Rachel okay?" I ask him. Rachel, Ryan's best friend since middle school, really adored Lexi before she fucked me over.

"I think so. She's torn up over it, like the rest of us." Ryan grunts. A door slams before he talks again. "They think someone murdered her."

I suck in a breath through my teeth.

"Yeah, man. They locked Xavier Hayes up. They're saying he did it. Who the fuck would do something like that?"

Drugs.

"I don't know," I mutter, scratching my cheek as I figure

out an appropriate response. Wouldn't be right to say *she did this shit to herself.*

But even I don't accept that, not one hundred percent.

"Listen," Ryan says quietly enough I almost miss it. "I just wanted to tell you since I know her family won't. Dickheads."

"Yeah. Thanks, man."

"You gonna get out to the show this summer?" He asks after a pause.

I smile and shake my head in disbelief. "Yeah, Ry. I'll come out there."

"Bring a girl or something, man." He laughs.

"Or something," I retort. Though he won't get what I mean.

"We miss you, Nix."

"I miss you guys, too. Honestly." I sigh and rest my hip against the railing as I watch everyone curl up on the couch below me.

"Probably won't see you at the funeral, then?"

"Probably not."

Why would I attend the funeral of a girl who tried to kill me?

"Well," he says, sighing. "See you sometime, Nix."

I hang up without responding and shove my phone back into my pocket.

My vision blurs from exhaustion, and the anger I've felt threatens to boil over. I need answers only Xavier Hayes can provide me.

It's time to go stare this fucker in the face.

"PHOENIX WEST," I say to the guard, showing my ID.

He looks over it, then looks up at me. "You're the kid whose family was murdered a year ago, ain't ya?"

I struggle not to roll my eyes as I frown and nod.

"Pity the girl was let off that easy." He hands my ID back to me and points to the lockers. "Put your stuff in there, and I'll let you back in a few minutes."

"Thanks." I walk over and put my keys and wallet inside a locker, locking it up when I'm done. My ass freezes off when I sit down in the plastic chair.

"Who you here to see?" the lady next to me asks.

I look up and meet her weathered gaze. "A friend."

"What are they in for?"

"I'd rather not say." I shift uncomfortably for the next few minutes, holding off her questions until the guard opens the door and lets a few of us inside.

When I enter the room, I immediately catch sight of Xavier Hayes and how haggard he looks.

I've never seen someone so young appear so rough and worn.

When I sit down, he flinches, and I cock my head to the side as I take in the bruises on his face. Someone's been beating the fuck out of him, and I almost feel bad.

"What do you want with me?" he asks. His voice is hoarse, as if he's not been using it, and he sounds so tired.

"What does Maxwell have over you?" I ask him, sitting straighter and clutching my hands together to keep from reaching over the table and punching his lights out.

"What?" He finally looks up from the table. His normally clear, ice-blue eyes are glassed over.

"Are you..." I scoff. "Are you fucking *high*?" I whisper the last part. For some reason, I don't want to get him into more trouble.

He snorts, flinching at his own noise, then shivers.

Holy fuck. He is.

"Stupid," I tell him. "That's really fucking stupid."

"Don't tell me about stupid. You left her all alone!" he snaps, glaring at me.

"She killed my family!" I whisper-shout.

He laughs, tossing his head back and earning us a glare from the guards.

"Shut the hell up and answer me." I snap, smacking the table.

"Nah," he says. "I won't tell you what he has on me. Shit's too much."

"Then tell me if you did this?" I wave my hand around. "Did you kill her?"

His eyes narrow as he stares me down, and his fists clench and unclench. "You honestly believe I'd kill someone I love?"

I shrug one shoulder. "Crimes of passion happen all the time."

He laughs again.

"Hayes!" a guard shouts. "Quiet down."

"Aye, aye, captain." He salutes the guy with his middle finger, and his handcuffs rattle with the movement.

"I need to know, Xavier," I tell him in a calm voice.

"Yeah, well," he grits out, glaring down at his hands.

I shift around as I wait for him to tell me more. When he

looks up at me with pain and unshed tears in his eyes, my breathing ceases.

"I didn't fucking do it. She took too many fucking drugs. I told her to stop. I begged her to stop. She had some of the new shit going around that fucking school and after about three pills, she started acting all fucking weird. At about number four in as many days, she was paranoid as hell and started puking. I didn't have a clue what the fuck to do. I took her ho-home." His breathing stutters and he buries his head in his hands. Red tinges his ears, no doubt in embarrassment.

"Shit," I mutter, slouching back in the chair and staring at his shaking shoulders.

"Five minutes!" a guard calls.

Xavier looks up at me and wipes his nose. "You're gonna get the fuck who made that shit, right?"

I nod once, unable to form any words.

"Good," he says, then blows out a breath. "I'm stuck here, I guess."

"Maxwell has shit on you that's that bad?"

He rolls his eyes before looking back at me. "Badder than bad, honestly. Doesn't help that Whitaker has a hold on shit here, too."

I wince and scrub a hand down my face.

"Do me a favor, man." He holds his hands up when I raise a brow at him. "You don't owe me one. But can you call someone for me? Make sure they're taking care of my gran? She's by herself."

I watch him for a beat, wondering if this would be worth my time. Not wanting to fuck my conscious over if I don't, I decide to help the old lady. "Fine," I grit out.

He rattles off a number, and I repeat it back a few times until I have it memorized.

The guard calls time for visitors, and I stand, looking down at Xavier.

"I think you'll get out of this, man. But," I huff out a laugh, "you're owed an ass beating from me. Don't forget it." I point a finger at him.

He shrugs and cocks a half-grin. "Fair enough, but I don't expect to get out of this shit alive. See ya."

I nod and turn, walking away from my ex-girlfriend's criminal ex-boyfriend.

It's like I'm in a dark romance novel or some shit.

I know I've told you I'm sorry about a
million times since the other night,
RaeRae… but… I really fucking am, okay?
Please stop shutting me out.

RAVEN

Get a fucking grip, asshole. Leave me
alone.

There's no excuse for what we did. At all.
Just know that I regret ever touching you.

Wait, that came out wrong.

RAVEN

River, leave me alone!

I regret ever touching you without your
express consent.

RAVEN

I'm so sorry you have regrets, River. Terribly
sorry. *eye roll emoji*

Take your anger out on me for as long as
you want. Just don't ignore me anymore.
Please?

RAVEN

middle finger emoji

I'll do anything you want me to do from
here on out until I prove how much I care
for you. I'm not gonna leave you alone. Not
now that I've had you.

Back to ignoring me? That's fine. I'll just
flood your texts with gifs of pineapples until
you respond.

raven

"That's the last of it," Pierce says as he tosses my tiny backpack into the front seat.

I smile gratefully up at him and stand to kiss his cheek.

Of course, that's not enough for him, so he grabs me around the waist and presses his lips to mine.

We have filled the last two weeks of the mundane with the magic of reigniting love. And perhaps budding love, too.

My heart skips a beat when Pierce traces his thumb along the exposed skin above my waist. I let my tongue trace his lower lip before I pull back, breathless.

He reaches up and twists a lock of my hair between his fingers before tucking it tenderly behind my ear. He grins that boyish grin that reminds me so much of our life before all of this.

"You ready for this trip, Blue?" he asks me, eyes boring into mine.

I nod and lean into his palm when he rests it on my cheek.

"Stop hogging her, pup. Just because you gained a temporary cease-fire while we go searching for the Florida sun doesn't mean you get to have her to yourself." River shoves Pierce out of the way and plants a kiss onto my lips. My toes curl in my boots.

"You realize I won her forgiveness over a video game, right?" Pierce grits out.

I shove away from River and climb into the Jeep, slamming the door and locking it before one of them can open it.

> You won my forgiveness because you told me the truth about the trafficking and where you found out about it. I don't have to accept your bullshit just because I love you. Let's go.

They read the text on Pierce's phone, then Pierce walks around the front and gets into the driver's side while River climbs in behind me. Phoenix is taking longer. Something about a call he had to make.

"You think he'll ever get over Lexi?" River asks.

I whip around and glare at him and sign; *He loved her at some point. You know that, right?*

He shrugs but folds his arms and looks out the window like a scorned child.

"Alright, well, who's choosing the music for the first leg of this drive?" Pierce asks. He taps the steering wheel and chews on his lip.

River and I almost butt heads when we reach for the controls on the stereo at the same time. My glare is enough to push him back in his seat, and I grin in victory as I turn on my current favorite radio station.

My music tastes change like the weather in the Midwest.

Never know what I'll vibe with or what will stick, but it's always changing.

Phoenix finally exits the garage, dressed in black jeans and a Henley stretched over his muscles. His jaw is tight, and he clutches his phone tightly in his fingers. When he sees us all staring at him, he stuffs it into his pocket and looks down at the ground until he makes it to the Jeep.

"Alright," he says after climbing in behind me. "Let's get going. Vegas is a long as fuck ways away."

"I've got it," Pierce tells him. Again.

Because this argument has been happening for over a week now.

Pierce insists he can drive the entire 12 hours straight through.

River swears we should stop and extend the trip one more day.

Phoenix wants to switch drivers halfway there for safety reasons.

I just want them to quit arguing for a change and act like adults.

Sighing, I rest my head back against the seat and close my eyes.

It's going to be a long week.

"I TOLD *you to take a damn left, Blue," Pierce yells at me. "Left. You took a fucking right."*

"There was no left, dumbass!" I shout at him, flailing my arms.

He grabs the steering wheel and growls.

Actually. Fucking. Growls.

"You're a damn animal, Pierce Jackson."

"I know you are but—"

I slam my foot onto the brake, put the car in park, and glare at him with my hands crossed over my chest.

"You can't stop in the middle of the road!" He tosses his hands up, runs them through his deliciously sweat-matted hair, down his face, then glares at me.

"You can't keep acting like a dumbass every single time someone else is driving a car."

"You're neurotic." He raises an eyebrow.

"You're infuriating." I raise one of mine back.

He launches forward and grips my jaw in between his fingers before slamming his lips to mine, and we groan in unison.

The cab of the car is suddenly too small. When Pierce rips both of our seatbelts off, I worry nothing would stop us at this point.

"Fuck," he breathes after breaking away from me, trailing his lips to my neck and nipping at the skin there.

"Green," I whisper.

It's no longer just his nickname.

It's the opposite of a safe word. It's our go-ahead word.

Our word that says I need more of you.

"We can't," he says as he slides his hand up my shirt and grips one of my breasts over my bra.

"You're right." I whimper when he pinches my nipple between his fingers, clenching my thighs in search of friction.

"We should get out of the road." He doesn't let up, sucking at my neck until it hurts deliciously.

"Mhm." I moan when he thrusts his other hand down my pants.

"You're a temptress of the worst sort, little bird." He groans in my ear when he shoves two fingers inside of me.

I'm soaking for him.

"I love when you call me that."

"Little bird?" he asks, pulling back to watch me.

I bob my head in a nod, because his thrusting fingers are bringing me to the brink and I can't think any longer.

"You gonna come for me, little bird?" He leans forward and places his lips near my ear, and I clench around him. "You gonna pop off so hard you soar into the clouds, baby girl?"

I whimper and nod, hiding my face in his neck and breathing in his scent.

He thrusts impossibly deep and grinds his palm against my clit, sending me spiraling into the orgasm I've desperately needed today.

The sounds that echo in the car would be embarrassing with anyone but him, and my body freezes as my climax takes over, my every nerve firing and colliding as I explode.

Once I've come down, he pulls his hand away, and I watch raptly, as he licks his fingers clean. Grinning when he catches me gawking at him, he leans forward and kisses me, shoving his tongue into my mouth and forcing me to taste myself. He threads his fingers in my hair, and I do the same to him.

A knock on the window startles us, and my head smacks on the side of the door when I flinch backward.

I rub the sore spot, wincing as I roll down the window. "After-noon, Sheriff," I flash him a sickeningly sweet smile.

"Ms. Hill. Mr. Jackson. Get your asses out of the middle of the road."

Pierce leans over me and tilts his head up, smiling up at the man. "Yes, sir." He presses the button to close the window and slides back into his seat.

I laugh loudly as I tear out of there, hoping like hell I never have to ask the Sheriff for a damn thing again since he's now seen my fresh-O face.

"You're embarrassing," I tell Pierce, faking a scowl.

"You're beautiful," he says.

"You..." I sigh.

"I love you."

"I love you too, Green," I reply, smiling when he rests his hand against the back of my neck and rubs small circles in my skin.

AS I WALK through the gas station, I yawn and rub sleep from my eyes.

We're stopped for maybe the fourth time. Didn't realize they had such weak bladders.

Grinning to myself, I reach over and snag a fudge round—or five—then head toward the drink coolers in the back.

"No circus peanuts, Blue?" Pierce asks as he steps up to my side. He leans forward and opens the fridge door and waits for me to grab a lemon lime soda.

Even though I could have opened the door for my damn self.

I sigh and shake my head at his question.

"I never thought I'd see the day you'd stop eating those damn things. They're nasty and you know it." He tosses his fist into the air before grabbing his own soda and walking toward the front to check out.

I grab a bag of circus peanuts out of spite and slap them

and the rest of my goods on the checkout counter, folding my arms.

Pierce rolls his eyes as he pulls out a card to pay for our stuff.

"Where you kids off to?" the clerk drawls.

"Florida," Pierce answers.

"Ah, typical spring breakers." The guy laughs. He tells Pierce the total and waits as he checks out. "Good luck to ya. Met my wife one spring break in Florida in '94. Best week of my life."

I wave at him as we leave, smiling. Once outside in the cool night air, I sigh wistfully and lean my head on Pierce's shoulder.

He wraps his arm around my shoulders and pulls me further into him as we walk toward the Jeep where River is pumping the gas.

"Nix not out yet?" River asks.

Pierce and I both shake our heads, looking back at the gas station to double check. My shoulders tense, but I take a deep breath and open my soda, sipping from it.

"We got, what, four or five hours left?" Pierce asks, yawning.

River nods and grabs his drink from the bag, cracks it open, and takes a sip. "I can take over. You need sleep."

Pierce shakes his head and smiles sleepily down at me. "You hear that, little bird?"

I raise a brow at him, and he rolls his eyes, tugging me into his chest. Now that I'm listening, I can hear the lyrics of A Moment Like This by Kelly Clarkson. It's a song we danced to countless times growing up, and I can't help but to rest my head against his chest and close my eyes.

As if he needs me even closer to him, Pierce wraps his

arms around me and kisses the top of my head and starts singing the lyrics about people waiting a lifetime for even one special moment. I know he's thinking of our love story and how we've gotten many of those moments in our lifetime. We're lucky to have our person here, and I'm even luckier to have River and Phoenix as my people, too.

He twirls me around and dips me low with his boyish grin shining in the midnight stars. My heart bursts with love for him. His eyes flit across my face before locking on my lips, and he kisses me as he brings me back up, his hands bunching in my shirt on my lower back.

I wrap my arms around his shoulders and allow him to push me back against the Jeep.

Pierce pulls back and presses his forehead against mine and inhales deeply, allowing us to breathe each other in for a few moments.

"I know this isn't what we originally had planned for The Great Road Trip," he whispers. "But can we pretend we're doing this for reasons other than some diabolical fuck who may try to kill off the whole campus?"

I nod, smiling when he does. His happiness is infectious. When he lets it show.

"I love you to the stars and beyond, little bird."

I get lost for a moment in those green eyes with my heart thundering in my chest.

He brushes his thumb across my cheek. "We're still forever, right?"

My heart skips a beat when I stare deeper into his soul, hoping not to make another mistake with him. Inhaling, I let out a long breath and nod, tightening my fingers in his shirt collar.

"Just gotta put me into that forever equation," River

butts in, kissing Pierce on the cheek before stealing me from between him and the Jeep. "Warm me up, RaeRae. I'm cold." He hugs me close and I wrap my arms around him, silently snickering as I watch Pierce flip him off behind his back. "I can feel that, pup. Keep it up and see what happens."

Pierce flips him off one last time before grabbing our bag of goodies and hopping into the driver's seat.

"Nix is coming back," River tells me, canting his head to the side as he looks over my shoulder.

I turn my head and watch Phoenix as he walks back toward the Jeep, coffee in one hand, phone in the other.

"He's so torn right now," River mutters, seemingly to himself. "Wanna sit in the back with him? See if maybe he just needs someone to listen? He won't talk to me."

I lift onto my toes and turn to kiss him on the cheek. *I'll get it out of him,* I sign.

River nods once, staring at Phoenix for a few more seconds before hopping into the front seat of the Jeep and slamming the door.

"Hey, Red," Phoenix says with all the false bravado he's been using on this trip so far.

I wave awkwardly at him as I lean against the back door.

"You sitting in the back with me?" he asks, his brows furrowing.

Is that okay? I sign.

"Absolutely." He leans in close to me, and just when I think he's going to kiss me, he opens the door and moves aside.

I frown as I climb inside, and River's brows furrow when he sees it in the rearview mirror. I shrug and he shakes his head, going back to eating his piece of beef jerky.

The door shuts harder than necessary as Phoenix climbs

in, and when we both have our belts done, Pierce drives back onto the highway.

I look over at Phoenix, seeing he's entranced in his phone again. Irritation prickles at me. I twist around and lean my back against the door, *accidentally* hitting his phone with my foot. It falls to the floor, and he growls before he can catch himself.

His face blanches, and he looks up at me. "Sorry, Raven."

I wince when he calls me by my name. He hardly does that.

"Do you need something?" he asks, sliding his hands along my ankles and playing with the edges of my sweatpants.

You're closed off, I sign. *Open up to me. I care about you and want to know how to help you through this.*

"There's nothing to get through."

The look I give him says it all, but I sign anyway. *Bullshit.*

He sighs and runs a hand through his hair before unbuckling his belt and mine and pulling me against him. He wraps his arm around my shoulders and twists our fingers together before kissing my head. "Listening to me talk about an ex-girlfriend is a weird kink, Red."

River snickers from his place in the front seat, and Phoenix kicks the back of it.

"Butt out," Phoenix snaps.

River nods and yawns, pulling his hood over his head as he leans against the door.

"I didn't really want her to die. She needed help. Death wasn't what I thought she needed." Phoenix sighs and lifts my hand, kissing each of my knuckles in a distraction to himself. "I don't know how to feel about any of this. And that guy, Xavier, being in jail for her murder, feels so wrong."

Do you believe him? I ask.

Phoenix told us about his visit with Xavier once he came back from the prison, looking worse for wear, and I knew it weighed heavily on him.

"I believe him. I don't know why, but I do. I'm upset he's being put on trial for shit he didn't do, but it seems like he has enough secrets to put himself away for a long time, if not on death row." He looks up to meet my gaze and the frustration lines every feature of his face. "I honestly don't want that for him. Maxwell has something to do with all of this, and so does Whitaker. This whole situation is fucked up, Red."

I nod and wrap my arms around his waist, resting my head against his shoulder where I can hear the pulse in his neck. It's so erratic my heart speeds up.

"I feel so fucked up in the head for being upset about her death, but I loved her at one point. Or at least I thought I did. It just fucking hurts. It all fucking—" his voice hitches and he buries his face in my hair, cutting off his words.

I stay like that with him for a while, allowing him a moment to grieve. I don't mention the tears which fall between us, nor do I mention how tightly he squeezes me until he falls into a heavy sleep, head lolling against his window as he snores.

River shrugs and I let out a long breath.

Grief may suck, and it may not make sense, but sometimes, we all need a moment to feel it.

pierce

My eyes droop for the umpteenth time as I drive back onto the highway toward Vegas.

With a few hours still left on this stretch, I don't know how in the hell I'm going to make it in one go, but Phoenix is a brooding dickhead, River's driving sucks, and I've never trusted Rae's. Ever.

The damn fender bender she got into with her car and the trashcan at fifteen was my first clue to her skills.

My lips kick up in a grin as I remember the absolute anger on her face as she scolded the trashcan, and a sleepy chuckle escapes me before I can catch it.

"You okay over there, Piercey Jackson?" River asks. He grabs his coffee and takes a big swallow.

I roll my eyes. He should be the last one with caffeine in hand at two in the morning. "Yeah. I'm good."

Movement catches my eye in the rearview mirror. For a second I think we're being followed, but blow out a breath when I catch sight of Rae and Nix's hands as they converse in ASL. I'm grateful we learned it for her, but when I can't watch them for fear of wrecking the car, I get a little frustrated.

I want to know all the thoughts in her pretty head. Whether they're on the same track as mine or somewhere else.

My thoughts are on forever, and I hope that's where she's at, too.

"So," River says, a shit-eating grin crawling its way along his lips.

I side-eye him and tap my fingers on the steering wheel.

"How the hell does this whole thing function in the real world? I've read up a bit on polyamory, and we could make this work. Are we in this for the long haul?"

"I am," Phoenix pipes up. "Rae just signed she is, too."

I meet his gaze in the rearview mirror, and he shrugs before pulling her into him. Biting my lip, I glance back at the road and watch the vast emptiness pass by us.

"I'm in it for as long as she'll have me," River states, reaching for his coffee. Again.

"Rae's always been my future, Riv. I've been gone for her since I was eight years old." I chuckle when her eyes meet mine in the rearview mirror, then wink before returning my gaze to the road again.

Something's not fucking right, and my gut is screaming at me.

"So then what? Do we just keep going the way we are now? Stay at Junk? Do we try to find a nice house to live in? What do you guys even want to do after college?" River continues to ramble, but I tune him out in favor of watching the black SUV behind us.

It's been following us for the last twenty miles and only

getting closer. I could have sworn I saw the same one at the gas station, too.

"River," I snap.

"What?" he asks, turning to sit properly in his seat. "I was just asking Rae what side of the bed she'd prefer to sleep on if we got a California king."

"Shut the fuck up," I tell him, slamming my hand on his chest as I swerve in front of a semi, attempting to hide from the SUV.

"The fuck!" Phoenix barks out, sitting up straight and strapping Rae and himself in.

"Someone's been following us." I blow out a frustrated breath and point toward my phone. "Call Lance."

"On it," River says. He pulls Lance's number up, putting it on the car speaker.

"I see him, Jackson." Thank fuck for Lance.

He's followed us since we left, with plans to watch our surroundings as we attempt to enjoy the trip down to Florida. He also has a team with him, though I can't see them. That little fact bugs me more than I'd like to admit.

"Who the fuck is it? Where did they come from?" I snap my questions out. The semi behind us blows his horn when I slow again.

The SUV passes by, then slows until they're able to keep up with us.

"Not a fucking clue, but we're running the tags. They started following from the gas station." Lance yawns, then groans. "Fuck. Can you take a damn break? We can take the next exit and—"

"No," I snap. "We're going through to Vegas and not stopping. Stop fucking asking." I peer over at River with narrowed eyes. "All of you."

Lance yawns again. "Fuck. Okay. Got it. Let me get on this guy's tail and push him into the next exit. Keep going, and I'll try to meet back up with you in a few miles." He hangs up, and the soft music which was playing before filters through the Jeep.

The SUV is still next to us, and I attempt to catch sight of who the fuck is in it, but the windows are illegally tinted, and it's pitch black outside. Lance's car gets close as fuck to the guy, practically nose to ass, then blares his horn loud enough we all jump. Panic floods my veins when the SUV almost swerves into us. I raise my brow, hoping the fucker can see it, and when Lance doesn't let up, they speed up.

I keep steady as Lance annoys the fucker enough that he ends up taking the off-ramp to the next exit, then grit my teeth and floor it.

"What the fuck?" River asks, grabbing the Oh-Shit Handle.

"Want to get as far from that fucker as possible, that's what the fuck." I grip the steering wheel until it creaks and don't slow until I sail past two more exits. "Text Lance and tell him what exit we just passed."

"Sir, yes sir," River snarks, releasing the handle and reaching for my phone.

"It's okay, Red," Phoenix croons from behind me.

I listen to the rustling of fabric as they settle back into their cuddle session, jealous he gets to have her warm body next to him.

"Alright, I got an idea." River only grins when I glare at him. "C'mon, we gotta release tension somehow. I want Rae to fall asleep with a smile on her face. Don't you?"

I nod once and set the cruise control for the Jeep again, relaxing as much as possible without endangering us.

"I spy with my—"

"Absolutely fucking not," I blurt out over his last few words.

"River," Phoenix groans, then yawns. "We're good back here. We're dead on our asses, anyway."

"Too soon, Nixy boy," River says as he turns around, pouting. "Too soon."

"Turn the music up back here," Phoenix says.

River does so, grumbling about party poopers.

Every so often, another car ends up behind us and I straighten, clenching the steering wheel tight all over again. At three in the morning, River yawns and looks over with this cocky looking grin.

"Hey, Pierce?"

"Hmm?"

"You ever think we're all gonna end up with a big ass wedding one day? Like she'd wear this big wedding gown, and all the people would be on her side of the aisle cause fuck us, right?" He chuckles and yawns again, covering it with his hand.

"Little different from what I'd..." I yawn. "Different from what I'd pictured as a kid. Stop yawning!" I scold him when he does it again.

"It's fuckin' hard not to. I'm tired." He looks back at Rae and Nix, a fond smile stretching his lips. "She's happy."

I shrug and chew my lip. "I hope so."

"Still don't wanna play I Spy?" He nudges my shoulder with his as he leans in close to me, the smell of his ocean-scented aftershave filling my nose.

"Nope."

"C'mon. I'll go first." He sits back in his seat. "I spy with my little eye—"

"Grow up, River," I snap, my voice harsher than I intended. I wince, about to apologize, when he glares at me. He hates when anyone tells him to grow up, and I've known that for long enough now to not get the same 'it's okay' when I say it.

"You know what, Pierce?" River snaps out, grabbing his earbuds and sliding them into his ears. "I grew up the moment Robert Jacobs stuck his dick up my ass. But thanks for the fucking reminder."

Rae gasps, and that's when I notice she's staring between us both in the rearview.

"Fuck," I whisper.

"Great," River says, glaring at the side of my head so hard it hurts. "Now she'll only look at me with pity. Thanks." He folds his arms over his chest and further pulls away from everyone, resting his head on the window.

I scrub a hand down my face and clench my jaw shut to avoid saying anything else stupid as fuck.

"I SWEAR TO GOD, RaeRae, it's gonna be the best night of our fucking lives," River says to Rae. He's turned around with his ass hanging in the air and I'm tempted to smack it.

Not a single person has fucking talked to me this morning. Not even at the gas station when I was trying to figure out what to do for breakfast an hour ago.

I keep fucking up, and I might be running out of chances with everyone.

Grunting, I turn left and check the rearview again.

Lance caught up with us an hour after he got the dick-head off the road, but hasn't called to inform me of anything. Which is frustrating. Trip would have told me everything in an instant.

I hate change, and changing body guards after half a year is a rough place to be in, because I have to rebuild trust with another person I don't know. Shit's hard enough when I don't know this person I've had blind trust for in the last four years.

His words come back to me: "It's a pity you're so young, but it's also a good thing. You get in and out of this shit, Jackson, and you'll be able to bring him to his fucking knees. You are the pillar of it all."

I don't know why I have to be the pin in this grenade.

Someone hated me enough in a past life to put me through all this.

"You passed the hotel," River tells me as he sits back in his seat. He doesn't look at me, keeping his gaze off me at all times.

"I want to make sure we aren't being followed."

"We aren't," Phoenix says. When I glare at him through the rearview mirror, he only glares in return. "Lance texted the group chat I started last night."

"We have a group chat?" I sigh and relax a bit in my seat.

"You kept all the information to yourself with Trip. This is not Pierce Steers the Ship anymore. So I made a group chat. May have to check your spam because your phone's dumb as fuck sometimes with groups." Phoenix throws his arm over Raven and kisses her temple.

My gut churns with jealousy, my ass hurts from sitting in this seat for so damn long, and my brain throbs with the need for rest.

I drive around the block again before pulling into the parking lot of our hotel. It's simple enough for our one-night stay here. I yawn when I park, tossing my head back on the headrest and stretching my fingers out.

"I checked us in," Phoenix says. "Texted you the room information and the code. You and Rae go ahead. River and I will grab the bags and meet you up there."

I should argue about him taking charge, but they keep saying they want more to do with the planning, so I'll let them have it. I push out of the Jeep, then open Rae's door.

She glares at me, and I don't have the energy to decipher why she's mad this time. I shut the door when she exits and follow, wondering if she'd be willing to help me blow off some of this fucking tension.

The death glare she settles on me as we enter the elevator says that's a no, so I lean against the opposite wall with my arms crossed and watch her as we're carried up to the fifth floor.

"Gonna hate me again, little bird?" I ask, raising a brow.

She flips me off and exits when the door opens, stomping off in the wrong direction.

"Other way, Blue." I chuckle when she spins around and stomps back in my direction. "Want to know the room number, or you gonna just keep throwing a fit?"

Huffing, she folds her arms and looks back at me with a raised brow.

"Five oh five." I point behind her, and she stomps off again.

My dick's hard, as it always is when her fire consumes us both. I know I won't get any attention in that regard, so I take a few deep breaths before following. Stepping up behind her, I cage her in with my chest to her back before leaning forward and punching in the room code. I open the door for her to step into, and sigh when she stomps into the bathroom and slams the door in my face.

I walk past her and take off my shirt and shoes before tossing myself onto one of the queen beds where sleep drags me under within seconds.

Fuck the drama. I'll deal with my fuckups after a recharge.

Probably.

Did you steal my panties from the bathroom?

RIVER

Uh… no?

Interesting, since I can't seem to find them. They were new, too! *sigh*

RIVER

Can I buy you new ones? What color do you want? Purple? Blue? Tangerine?

Is tangerine even a color?

RIVER

Fuck yeah it is. And it'd pop against your skin, too!

You do realize I see the panties hanging out of your back pocket right now, right?

Don't give me that look, River Jacobs. They're mine.

RIVER

I'll buy you a whole new set if you let me keep these. *puppy dog eyes emoji*

Fine, but they better be good quality.

RIVER

Fuck yes! Also, thank you for spending time with me earlier. I hope we have many more nights just like that. Maybe add a guy or two.

If you're okay with it, that is. You have to be okay with everything we do or we don't do it.

Also, if you want… I really want to dance with you again at tomorrow's party. That okay?

Depends on what type of panties you find me.

RIVER

Bet.

raven

After watching Pierce sleep for about an hour, I curled up against him, resting my head on his chest and wishing I could confess all of my secrets to him while he slept. He couldn't respond, nor would he even remember what I confessed in this state, but at least my secrets would be out there, somewhere. Out of my head.

I hadn't meant to fall asleep, but being in a car for over twelve hours exhausted me. It was a foregone conclusion that we'd all fall asleep.

River and Phoenix came in over three hours ago and also fell asleep, their soft snores lulling me into a comfort I didn't know I needed.

"Fuck," Pierce groans from beside me, wrapping his arm around my waist and pulling me into him. "You smell so fucking good, little bird."

My core heats, but I ignore it in favor of sitting up and placing my hand in his hair, running my fingers through his scalp.

He groans and sighs. "I'm sorry," he whispers.

I tug until he looks at me, then I pull my hands away so I can sign. *Apologize to River, not me. You were such an ass to him last night.*

He sighs and buries his face in my chest. "I know. No excuses," he grumbles, looking up at me. "You doing okay after hearing that?"

I shrug and bite my lip, my gaze flitting over to River before looking back at Pierce and nodding.

"He's okay. It hasn't happened in a while." Pierce sighs and rests his cheek on my chest, looking over at the man in question, splayed out with his leg half hanging off of the bed and his hair plastered to his face.

I thread my fingers through Pierce's hair and rest my head back on the pillow.

"We should get up. Clean up." Pierce sits up and stretches his arms above his head before sliding off of the bed. With an extended hand, he grins and all that boyish charm I fell in love with bleeds from him. "Will you shower with me, little bird?"

I chew my lip, debating the consequences of doing so, then shrug and grab his hand. My head falls back on a laugh when he yanks me up and sweeps me into his arms. He carries me bridal style to the bathroom and kicks the door shut behind us. My heart hammers in my chest when he pushes my back against it, the snick of the lock a definitive barrier between us and the other two.

"Can I have just a few minutes of your time all to me, Blue?" Pierce asks, leaning in until our noses brush. "I want to spend time with just us. If this," he swallows hard enough I hear it, "if this arrangement with the guys is gonna work, I only ask that you let me have you alone from time to time." He looks up at me from beneath his long lashes—seriously, why do guys get longer natural lashes than girls do—and licks his lips. "Is that something we can agree to? You can work in alone time with them, too. I don't mind sharing, but I get greedy for you, baby."

I take a deep breath and smile before nodding once.

"Can I kiss you, Blue?"

My heart threatens to give out. I'll forever be grateful he's asking for my permission now. I nod and exhale a shaky breath when he collars my throat and slams his lips against mine as if we flipped a switch and he can no longer wait for me.

He groans as he leans his body against mine, grinding every hard ridge he can manage against me. He threads his fingers in the hair at the base of my skull, tugging to control the angle of my head, and I grasp at his shoulders, my nails digging into his skin.

I can't remember the last time I spent time with just him, and it definitely feels overdue after all the shit we've been through.

He breaks from our kiss and pulls back, chuckling when I frown. He crooks his finger as he backs into the shower and turns the water on before stripping out of his pants and underwear. I watch as he strokes his cock a few times, grinning when he sees me staring at him with my lip caught between my teeth.

I strip my own clothes off and toss them into the pile he started, then climb in. Shivers wrack my frame and goosebumps rise along my skin from the temperature difference, but that could also be how turned on I am by the way he's pumping his hand over his dick while his eyes devour every inch of me.

"I want to fuck you into the tiles of this shower, Raven," he says, voice low and husky.

I raise a brow in challenge at him, chewing on the inside of my cheek as I move my eyes up his frame until I meet his gaze.

"But I don't feel right getting your pussy without them here. So you're gonna stand on one end of the shower, and I'll stand on the other. Then we're gonna get ourselves off."

I roll my eyes.

"Our future can start on this trip, Blue." He groans as he pumps his hand a few more times. "I don't want to piss anyone off anymore."

He says such pretty words.

I grin and nod, leaning my back against the opposite shower wall. My hips buck forward when my hand descends, my fingers connecting with my swollen clit as I watch him hungrily.

"Fuck," he groans.

My breathing grows heavy as I watch him, my thighs trembling when I shove my fingers inside my wet cunt as I watch him watch me.

It feels like we're straddling a fine line we didn't know we drew until now, and the temptation to cross it is enough to make my pussy clench around my fingers. A long breath leaves me and I meet his hooded gaze as I trail my other hand down to my chest, pinching and playing with my nipples until his jaw clenches.

"I'd haul you up that wall and fuck you senseless, little bird. I'd impale you on me so far you wouldn't know where you started and I ended."

My head falls back, and I keep my eyes on him as I add in an extra finger. Biting my lip, I grind my clit against my palm, pumping my fingers at the same furious pace he's pumping over his dick.

"I remember how fucking amazing you felt when we all took you. River's dick in your ass, Nix in your mouth." Pierce groans and stills his hand for a second, his back arching as he stares at me. "You've turned into such a filthy slut and I'm obsessed with you more because of it."

My eyelids flutter closed with his words, imagining Valentine's Day and how absolutely filthy we got. A dream come true for a girl like me. My thighs shake again at the memory, and I grip the small handrail to keep from falling.

"Gonna come for me, baby?" Pierce groans when I nod. "Give it to me, Raven. Come so hard you see all the pretty stars in the sky."

I open my eyes and meet his gaze just as I crest over the edge, plunging into an orgasm so beautiful, yet muted in the way it suspends us both in time. I watch as his cum falls to the floor beneath us, wishing he'd have let it land on me instead.

He walks forward and engulfs me in a kiss before pulling my fingers to his mouth, tasting me. His nostrils flare before he grunts and pulls back, thrusting himself into the water. A grin creeps along his lips, and he cocks his head to the side. "I love watching you fall apart to filthy words, Blue."

I glare at him and playfully nudge him out of the water, then spend the next twenty minutes hogging it until it runs cold, leaving him to cool down. He needs to stop turning me on because we don't have enough time in the world to satiate ourselves.

He reaches out from behind the shower curtain and

swats me on the ass with a playful growl, and I kiss him one last time before leaving the bathroom with the dumbest grin on my face.

I'm met with the smell of burgers and fries the second I open the door, as well as the hungry looks of my other two insatiable neanderthals. I cock a brow at them both as I walk to my suitcase and grab some underwear, then snatch one of their hoodies from the bed and toss it over my frame.

"She teases," River says, laughing when I stuff a fry in my mouth. "Suck on that fry some more, baby. Give me something for the spank bank."

I thrust the fry in and out of my mouth for his amusement, and Phoenix rolls his eyes, though his lips kick up in a small grin against his will.

"What'd you two do in there, RaeRae?" River asks, adjusting the bulge in his sweats.

Rocket science, I sign. When he raises a brow, I shrug. I point toward the double bacon cheeseburger, blowing a kiss when he hands it over.

As I take my first bite into the glorious grease and carbs, I plop down onto the bed next to Phoenix, trying to catch a glimpse of his phone as he types away on it with furious and fast-moving fingers. I'm not worried about him fucking around on me–us–but he's been so distracted I don't know if he notices half of what's going on around him anymore.

Which worries me, since he's usually so *on* all the time.

Phoenix clears his throat and shoves his phone in his pocket, and looks over at me. He reaches for his own fry and bites into it, his gaze sweeping over me. "You like stealing all of our clothes, Red?"

I shrug and take another bite of my burger, eyes locked on his.

He shakes his head, but just as he's about to speak, Pierce exits the bathroom and walks to his suitcase, grabbing a pair of fresh sweats and underwear. He changes and looks around at the food, grinning when he sees me eating.

Pierce grabs a burger and tears into it. After eating the first bite, he sits next to River and points at everyone. "We need to have a talk."

Phoenix sighs and grabs his own burger, and River rolls his eyes.

"What the fuck are we doing in this relationship? We haven't talked about it, and it's bugging me." Pierce licks his lips, then looks at Phoenix. "I'm serious about her, and I don't want anything to fuck this up."

"Well, you could stop being a dick for a change." Phoenix raises a brow when Pierce clenches his jaw shut. "But I'm in it for the long haul. I'm good with all that we've done, and so long as no one goes *hogging our girl,* I don't mind whatever happens." He wraps an arm around my shoulders and kisses my temple. "So long as she's happy, I'm good."

"I'm good with everything, too," River says through a mouthful of food.

I wrinkle my nose and look back at Pierce, who looks confused.

"Why did I think this would be a harder conversation?" He sighs and runs a hand through his hair before looking at me. "I want it to be a stepping stone for us. This is where I want to call this official. I'm in this for good, Rae. You know that as much as anyone else. We're yours." He grins sheepishly and shrugs. "So long as you want us."

I nod and stand, smiling around at all of them. *Are you*

saying you guys want to be boyfriends and girlfriend now? Officially?

Pierce rolls his eyes and bites into his burger, glaring at me.

Joke's on him because that glare is hot as hell.

"Why are we even having this conversation?" Phoenix asks.

"Because I want to draw lines in the sand. Around us. I don't want anyone to get the wrong idea, and we've never had this conversation. We've just assumed." Pierce sighs.

We're good. I like this, and I don't think we need a schedule or anything, just be conscious of the time spent. Going with the flow is best, I think, I sign, shrugging at the end before grabbing my burger and biting into it again.

All three of the guys nod and I grin.

"What are we doing tonight, anyway?" River asks, stuffing a fry in his mouth.

"I got us all tickets to go to this speakeasy slash night-club," Phoenix says. He stands and walks over to his bag, grabbing his wallet from the side pocket. "With that in mind. We need suits, gentlemen."

I fold my arms over my chest and stare at him, a small smile threatening my lips.

"And you'll get yourself a pretty dress, Red." Phoenix holds up a black Amex and my brows shoot up. "Don't ask. Our mutual contact has all the best connections."

"Wait. *He* got you an Amex?" Pierce shoots to his feet. "I fuckin' asked him to get me shit like that years ago."

Phoenix shrugs, and a wicked grin pulls at his lips, a playful glint in his eyes. "Guess he likes me better."

Who's he? I sign.

"We don't fucking know," Pierce snaps, still glaring daggers at Phoenix.

"Alright," River says, standing. "Simmer down. Let's take the lady shopping, shall we?"

"STUFF me in another shitty suit and I'll kill you so slow you won't know when the pain will end, Nix," Pierce snaps, tossing another jacket over the changing room door.

I catch it and put it back on the hanger to avoid any 'you break it, you buy it' fees.

The suit is worth five thousand dollars, and Pierce hates it.

I roll my eyes and grab another one, more suited to his attitude than his body. Just so happens when he tries *this* one on... it looks like sin on him.

"Better." Pierce adjusts the cuffs of the black shirt before sliding the jacket over his frame.

I shift in my seat as the other two walk out in matching suits, salivating and wanting to take a bite from each of them.

River winks, annoyingly sweet, as he brushes a hand through his freshly cut hair. It's longer in the front, the hair brushing over his eyebrows, and shorter toward the back. While I'll miss having more strands to hang on to while his face is between my thighs, it makes him look older. And an older River will be nothing to scoff at, I'm sure.

Phoenix walks out of his stall wearing a black on black suit, much like the one he wore at the party when I first showed up at Cobalt University, and I clench my thighs together. His black hair is up in its signature bun, and he scratches his hand across his day-old stubble, a scowl stretching his lips.

You look fine, I sign, and he relaxes his shoulders a little.

Pierce looks over at me and tilts his head. "Are we up to your standards, Blue?"

With a roll of my eyes, I stand and walk around all of them, sliding my hand up Phoenix's chest. My fingers tingle as I trail them up River's arm, and as I step toward Pierce, I run my gaze from his toes to his face, biting my lip. I look up at him through my lashes and my breathing picks up when his nostrils flare. Both of my hands slide up his arms until they cross behind his neck, and I lift on my toes to press a gentle kiss onto his lips. When I playfully nip at him, he growls and the sound travels through my entire body.

"Filthy little vixen," River snickers, sliding behind me and shifting my hair from my shoulder and nipping at the juncture between my neck and collarbone.

"Gentlemen," the clerk calls, clearing his throat. "I must ask you to refrain from these activities in the shop."

"Our apologies," Phoenix says, glaring at the other two, though I don't miss him adjusting the tent he's pitching in his own pants.

We leave after buying the suits for the boys, and head to another shop full of dresses.

Upon dresses.

Upon dresses.

I gape up at one wall of little black dresses, wondering why each one increases in price when their designs are the same.

"You'd look gorgeous in any of them," Phoenix says as he

wraps his arms around my waist. "Pick one, Red, and we'll make sure it gets dirty tonight."

My entire body shivers, and he chuckles in my ear, tightening his hands on my waist before letting me free and going to sit down on the couch where the other two are bickering over something. Again.

They fight like an old married couple, and it warms my heart.

"Are you looking for something in particular?" a girl asks as she steps up beside me.

I gesture toward the wall and she lets out a small laugh, walking toward the one on the lower shelf.

"With your figure, and those boys? This is definitely made for you." She holds the dress out to me and I grab it, pretending I did *not* see the price tag.

A thousand dollars for a dress I might wear only once is absurd for anyone, but especially someone who grew up in poverty and now has access to a fucking Amex card attached to who-knows-who's bank account.

I walk into the changing room stall, then close and lock the door so none of the boys can get us into trouble.

I just might let them.

A grin stretches my lips. I'm just as culpable as they are in most of our shenanigans. I tear off my shirt, shorts and shoes before pulling the dress on over me. Thank god it's one I just have to pull over my head. Having to do up a zipper on the back of a dress is its own brand of torture. The silky material molds to me like a second skin and dips between my cleavage, showing off the small roundness of my breasts. The sides are cut-outs, exposing the skin underneath with strands of material crisscrossed down the sides until they reach my hips.

I feather my hands up along my body until I reach the small spaghetti straps, tracing them to where it exposes my skin, only covering my ass and part of my lower back.

A small smile tilts my lips as I meet my blue eyes in the mirror.

The boys are going to die.

Once I've redressed and put the dress back on the hanger, I walk toward the counter and pull the Amex out of my pocket to pay for it. The clerk tries to talk to me, but I act distracted to avoid the way most people end up yelling in order to talk to me.

I'm mute, not deaf, but sometimes people can't differentiate the two.

I nod in thanks when she hands me the bag, then I walk back over to the boys. Instead of stopping, however, I walk right past them, just to see if they'll follow *me* for a change.

A grin splits my face when they fall into a line behind me.

"So," River says, impatient. "What'd you get? Wanna show the class?"

I shake my head and pull the bag closer to me.

"She'll show us soon enough," Pierce says, stepping up to my side and throwing an arm around my shoulders.

"We have an hour to get back to the hotel, get changed, and get into the speakeasy," Phoenix says.

So, that's exactly what we do.

I NERVOUSLY APPLY blood-red lipstick before walking out of the bathroom and showing them what I chose.

You could hear a pin drop with how quiet the room becomes when I enter.

"Do we have to leave?" River asks as he adjusts himself in his slacks.

I smile and nod at him, holding out my arms and twirling for all three of my boys.

I've never felt so much like a princess in my life... and a vixen at the same time, because they'll eventually figure out I don't have any underwear on underneath this.

"Dammit, this is going to be uncomfortable now," River complains again. He walks over to me and wraps me in a warm hug, kissing along my neck as he holds me in front of the other two. "You're so fucking gorgeous, Rae."

"Alright, alright," Pierce says. "Let's go before I decide to stay in."

"You need to remember you don't make all the decisions anymore, Pierce." Phoenix smacks him on the back of his shoulder as he passes. He brings me out of River's hold and kisses my forehead before grabbing my hand and tugging me out of the hotel room.

"Why the hell are we walking?" Pierce grumbles as we walk along the busy sidewalk a few minutes later.

"It's around the corner," Phoenix tells him.

I'm lost in the sights and sounds of Vegas, hoping we get a chance to come back in a few years when we're a little older. A little less stressed. I'd love to gamble away my last dollar just to see if I strike it big.

"This is a museum," River says, pointing at the sign above the Mob Museum.

"Have faith, gentlemen." Phoenix grins, opens the door wide for me, and gestures me inside. "After you, my lady."

"You sound like an old man, Nix." Pierce grunts when Phoenix punches him in the gut before placing his hand on the small of my back.

As we shuffle inside, I'm lost reading news articles about the mob, taking in the outfits and differences in each.

It fascinates me how a large group of criminals can be so powerful, yet remain hidden to so many people. Makes me wonder what people miss if they aren't looking something directly in the eye.

"Come on," Phoenix says, waving us over to a corner. He leans toward a suitcase and spins it.

My heart skips a beat.

The wall moves backward and reveals a staircase.

"Okay," River says, grinning. "That's fucking cool."

I nod, smiling up at Phoenix, who has his eyes locked on me. I take his hand and he leads me down the stairs into the speakeasy.

The room is dark, lit only by small sconces every few feet and oil lamps on each table. Red cloths cover each table, intricate and elaborate designs woven into each one. The floor is black carpet, except for the spot in front of the stage set for dancing, which is a black marble. String lights line the rounded outer rim of the dark wood stage where the blood red curtains are closed, and people mill about.

I'm stunned.

When we pause next to the bar, I look up at Phoenix and sign, *This looks straight out of a movie.*

"Be careful, the mob boss might hear you say that and capture you, princess." Phoenix grins at my shocked face, then orders us all drinks and hands them out. He holds a martini glass toward me and I raise a brow in question. "I know you've never had one. This trip is for new experiences, right? I want to try as many new things with you as I can."

I nod and take the drink from his hand, slipping my other around his waist as we walk toward the table Pierce and River have claimed as ours in one of the back corners.

As much as we all enjoy going out and doing things, we know our social limitations.

"Ladies and gentlemen! If you would please turn your attention to the main stage. We have a guest with us tonight. Olivia Hunter!"

"Wait, Nix," Pierce sits up straighter, adjusting his bowtie. "Isn't that—"

"Yep," Phoenix says, his eyes glued to the stage where the curtains part and reveal a gorgeous woman.

"Holy fuck," River whispers, leaning over the table as if the extra one foot of distance will help him see her clearer.

"Hello, everyone," she speaks through the microphone. "I'm here to entertain you tonight, so I hope you're ready. I'm taking a spin on some new songs, turning them into tunes of the twenties. Please," she smiles as she looks out over the crowd, "enjoy."

"Come dance with me?" River asks me, already standing.

I take a sip of my martini–it's not *so* bad–and stand, placing my hand in his.

We'll leave Phoenix to his thoughts again.

River escorts me onto the dance floor, wrapping one arm around my waist until his palm lands flat on the skin of my lower back. He captures my other hand in his as he sways, then steps with me. His eyes bore into mine as we listen to a twist on Shut Up and Dance by Walk on the Moon.

"Keep your eyes on me," River sings alongside the woman on stage. "You're holding back."

I mouth the words with him, grinning as our gazes meet. *Shut up and dance with me.*

The soft tunes make the song more of a ballad than the catchy pop single it is, and my heart skips several beats as I watch River Jacobs transform in front of me. He started off this dance as someone who just wanted to touch me, to someone who can't let me go.

I'm not sure I ever want him to.

His jacket is cold against my palms as I slide them up his shoulders until my hands cinch together behind his neck. He brings me closer to him, my chest to his, and dips his head lower, keeping those eyes locked with mine.

"Rae," he whispers.

My eyes cast between his lips and his eyes, and before he can say anything else, I sever the last thread between us and press my lips to his, drowning out any words.

Words hurt when people use them.

There's clapping all around us as the song ends, only to go quiet again when another song starts. River holds me there, kissing me, whispering sweet nothings into my ear as we dance for hours. Phoenix joins us, but his jaw is tight and there's tension clear in how his posture never relaxes.

Closer to eleven, Pierce comes up and steals me away, spinning me in circles along the dance floor with the wildest grin on his face.

"Hey," he says, leaning down to kiss me as I try to take a breath from all the dancing. "So I was thinking, when we go back to the hotel—"

I nod, biting down on my lip as I imagine all the filthy scenarios the boys could get up to in a hotel room with me.

"We could—" Pierce winces and reaches into his suit jacket pocket, his brows furrowing when he checks the caller. His eyes meet mine and he kisses my nose. "I'll be back."

Then he leaves the speakeasy.

There's only one person he would take a private call with...

Maxwell fucking...

pierce

"Langston?" I ask, already frustrated because I had all the best filthy thoughts of my girl ripped from my head just now.

"Jackson," he says, slurring my name. "I dunno what to do, boy. I really don't."

"About what?" Like I have no fucking clue what's going on.

"You. My daughter. The other two boys. What will Robert Jacobs think about his son mucking up his Christian reputation by screwing around with another man, huh?" Maxwell laughs, and I curse under my breath. "You fucked with me too much, Jackson."

"I don't have a damn clue what you're talking about." Lies. I know everything. *Almost* everything.

Maxwell's laugh grows louder, as though I've told him the best joke ever. A violent cough interrupts him, and he groans when he's able to breathe again. "Where did you take my daughter, Jackson? Hmm?"

"Doesn't matter. It's spring break."

"Oh, it fucking matters." I make out the telltale sound of a lighter flicking open in the background. "Her future husband wants to know where his property is."

"She'll never be his property!" I kick the brick wall outside of the museum, grunting in pain.

"Oh, I know." He chuckles darkly. "She'll always be mine. I think I'm going to set her up in a room and let a few men have at her. She likes the group activities, anyway. Maybe I'll film it."

"You're fucking sick, Langston." I bite back any other response I have.

"You've been at my side for so long, Pierce. I know you. You won't let harm come to her. You should hand her over. Hmm? You can make all of your other shit right that way. I can keep her safe."

"Safe isn't parading her around in front of dozens of other sick old men who get off on taking young girls!" I hiss.

"Safe also isn't taking her out of this state and putting her at risk of being snatched up by random strangers in tourist hot spots!" Maxwell bellows. "I'm giving you until the end of the week to return my daughter to me. Then I'm coming for you and your friends, and you won't like what I have planned for you, boy."

He hangs up, and I shove my phone into my suit jacket so hard I worry the pocket might bust. Tossing my head back, I stare up at the foggy night sky and exhale a harsh breath.

I need to get fucking drunk.

"PIERCE!" River yells over the sound of the newest song.

"What is it, Master?" I slur out, grinning when his eyes flare wide. "Fuck yes, you love when I call you that, and I love when you call me pup. Hey, Blue," I say, leaning toward Raven, only she's a lot closer and I push her back into her chair by accident. Shit.

"I think you've had enough, Pierce," Phoenix says. His face turns stony and grumpy.

I reach up and smash his lips together, trying to make him smile. "Why don't you smile?" I ask him. "She likes you the most, y'know. Probably cause she's the only one you stick your dick into."

Still forcing the smile on Nix, I lean to the side and pout at my little bird. With my free hand, I point to River. "You mad I stick my dick in this guy?"

Raven rolls her eyes, then shakes her head and signs something.

It doesn't make sense though, so I nod eagerly and kiss her lips before floating away with River until we're outside on the sidewalk. He teleported us with magic!

"It's fuckin' cold, man," I complain, leaning against River's shoulder. "How's it cold in Vegas?"

"Your temperature's all fucked, pup. You're sloshed." River's arm tightens around my shoulder and I sigh.

"I'm not a sloth. I'm a trash panda."

River laughs. "Why would you be a trash panda?"

"Cause I create a lot of fuckin' problems for people. Like trash pandas." I trip over something. I think it was a crack in the sidewalk trying to beat my face in. "It's fine though, cause I'm cute, right?"

"Alright man, we need to get you back to the hotel."

"Raven wants to go to this club," Phoenix says, sounding so far away. Why's he so far away?

"I'll take Pierce back," River says, and I groan.

"Fuck that, I wanna go to the club, too!" I whine, looking up at River with what I hope are convincing puppy dog eyes.

River glares at me for a moment, then sighs and turns us around.

"He can't drink anything else," Phoenix orders, pointing at me. "He's going to get alcohol poisoning."

Raven's pretty blue eyes stare at me and I grin at her like a dumbass, thinking about all the ways I wish I could show her I love her if we were a normal ass couple in a normal ass setting without some stupid evil Maxwell Langston lording over us.

"Hear that, pup?" River says in my ear, and I jump, almost smashing my head into his face.

"Huh?"

"You drink water here. That's it. We don't want you dying on us."

I grin and try to stand straighter as we walk through the door of this club.

It's so fucking loud in here I can't even hear my own thoughts.

Fuck. Yes.

I step behind Raven and wrap my arm around her, nudging her to the dance floor and away from Daddy Nix and Master River. "Dance with me, little bird? Please?"

She doesn't look back at me, and that fucks with me more than I'll ever admit, but she does lean her body into mine, swaying with me as I move us to the music.

My hands dig into her hips as I grind against her, claiming her right on the dance floor for all to see. I bend down and place sloppy kisses on her bare shoulder and neck, groaning when the smell of strawberry soda invades my senses. "I love you so fucking much."

Her body stiffens, but she relaxes when I kiss her again.

"Let me fuck you tonight, little bird?" I ask her. Beg her. "I want to bury myself in you so deep, I won't know which way is up and all my problems disappear."

She turns in my arms, scowling up at me for a moment before she shakes her head and rushes away.

My jaw drops and I open my arms wide, staring after her. "What the fuck?" I yell.

But no one can fucking hear me over the sound of the club music.

River moves to my side, throwing a rough arm around my shoulders and pulling me in tight. "How'd you piss her off this time?"

"I said I wanted to be buried so far inside of her that all my problems would disappear."

"I see." He chuckles and tugs me off to the side toward a table, forcing me into a chair. "Drink this." He hands me a bottle of water.

I grimace and uncap it, then chug half of it in one go. I won't admit how good it feels instead of the burn from all the alcohol I've already had.

"Do you know why you keep fucking up, Pierce?"

I snap my gaze to meet his and shake my head.

"You keep making sex a priority. You keep acting like she's required to make you feel better by letting you have her body." River holds up his hands when I try to object. "Listen. She's not an object, man."

"I know that!"

"Then fucking treat her like the queen she is and stop

objectifying her. Her pussy is great, sure, but it's her soul that sings to us, and you know that more than anyone. Hell." He scoffs, running a hand through his sweaty hair. "Man, we've known her for less time than you, yet Nix and I see how her soul is searching for the freedom she deserves. When she gets it, do you really think she's not going to fucking run from us? We can't hold her down. We can only beg whoever runs the universe to let her bring us with her wherever she goes."

"River, I—"

"We have a fucking problem," Phoenix says, stepping up to our table. His jaw clenches tight and his eyes fill with rage.

"The fuck's going on, Nixy-boy?" River asks, patting his shoulder. He glares one last time at me, as if I hadn't already gotten the point.

I nod once and finish my water bottle before turning to look where they are.

Raven is on the dance floor. Our caged little bird.

Dancing with other men.

Four of them, to be exact.

They're crowded around her, smirking over her shoulders at each other as she throws her arms in the air. One has her hips in his hands. Another grabs her wrists and rests them on his neck. The other two block her in, and my gut twists as one holds up a bag with something tiny inside and the other nods.

"Nix—"

"Let's go," he growls. He pushes through the crowd as fast as possible, with River and me behind him.

As drunk as I am, I still stand tall and fold my arms over my chest as I stare down the group of men who thought it was okay to take our little bird out for a spin and drug her.

"Gentlemen," Phoenix says.

"Hey man," one douche says. "You up to party with her, too?"

"Actually—" River pipes up, but Phoenix pinches him in the side.

"What kind of party are we having with all of you and only one of her?" Phoenix's question makes me straighten my spine as my gaze shifts between the four guys.

"A train, man. She's already so fucked. Give her a little *fun candy* and she'll be ready to do whatever we want. Huh, sweetheart?" He tilts Raven's chin up, and I see the panic in her eyes clear as day.

She had no clue what she was getting into when she tried to dance with these guys.

"Here's where you're wrong," Phoenix says.

"Wrong?" one guy asks, as if he hasn't been wrong a day in his life.

"You see, gentlemen," Phoenix leans forward, his hands stuffed into his pockets. "Red? Yeah. She's with us. Has been for a while now, and I'd like it if you took your filthy fucking hands off her before I rip them off." He stands tall again, glaring down his nose at them all.

"Why did she come dance with us if she was with you?"

"Because we fucked up," I tell him, meeting Raven's gaze. "But we're here to apologize and to beg for forgiveness." I stare at the guys again. "Something you fuckers look like you don't give a shit about."

Raven tries to escape while the men are distracted, but one of them grips her by the bicep. I growl when she winces.

"I don't think we'll give her up. She wanted a fun time,

she found it. Simple." This fucking guy shrugs like we're talking about a toy and not a human being.

Fuck, River was right about me treating her like an object. I'm a dickhead.

The bouncer comes by and narrows his eyes when he catches sight of the one with his hand on my girl. "Is there a problem here?"

Phoenix grins, then points to Raven. "They've been holding our girl hostage and are planning to drug her. Might want to check their pockets. Make sure they don't have any other drugs on them."

The bouncer steps forward, and all four of the fucks give him a wide berth, releasing Raven.

She rushes headfirst into Phoenix, burying her face into his chest just as hell breaks loose behind her.

While I wish she'd have rushed into my arms, at least she's safe with someone who cares for her.

I meet River's gaze and he nods toward the front of the club, indicating we leave this fucking place.

Fine by me.

Hey sweet girl.

RAERAE

What's wrong?

Nothing. I hope.

RAERAE

I'm just tired.

Tired people don't try and jump out of
moving vehicles, RaeRae.

RAERAE

I blacked out. PTSD fucks with my head
daily.

It was scary to watch you like that. Not
gonna lie. I was terrified.

RAERAE

If we're all doing this long term… it'll have
to be something you get used to.

I can take whatever you throw at me, baby.

That was rude!

RAERAE

laughing emoji You said you could take
whatever I throw at you!

Your fucking shoe wasn't what I had in
mind.

RAERAE

Alright alright. I'm not sorry because it was
funny AF.

You, me, Mario Kart. Ten minutes.

RAERAE

You think you can beat me?

I know I can.

RAERAE

Convince the others, then. It's on!

After we get through this next box.

raven

I only meant to piss Pierce off when I left to dance with the other guys, but by the third song, things got a little hazy.

The drink they handed me was all sorts of fucked up. I was grateful I noticed it by the second sip, and not the second glass.

They started touching me subtly at first, but they turned more confident and obvious. I avoided being drugged with the pill they were handling, but my skin and brain seemed as though they were on fire and my body became looser the longer I hung around them.

So I danced.

I knew the boys would be watching. That they'd get me out of the trouble I'd found myself in.

Just took them longer than I'd expected.

My nose is all stuffed up from crying. I blow it into a napkin Phoenix got me as we were on our way out of the club.

We're close to the hotel, and it's so quiet. I hate it. The

city is loud and bright as hell. Still going strong at... is it one or... two in the morning now?

"Stupid, Red," Phoenix mutters, and I wonder if he meant to even say it out loud.

I look up at him and nod. I know what I did was Stupid Bitch 101.

I was begging for trouble when I left in search of a group of guys much like my own. Problem is, I'd already survived the worst of my own boys. No need to survive the same from strangers.

"Be nice," Pierce says. He still slurs his words.

Phoenix snorts and shakes his head as we enter the hotel lobby. He escorts us to the elevator and we all step on, then stand in silence until it opens back up on our floor.

"You okay?" he asks as we walk a few feet behind the other two.

I nod and chew my lip as Pierce and River enter the room, my pulse rising the closer we get.

"You deserve a punishment for that shit," Phoenix growls in my ear as we step inside. He closes the door, and I jump when he grabs me by the hips. "Do you know what the hell it feels like to watch you willingly go into someone else's arms? Are we not enough for you, Raven?"

You're more than enough, I sign to him. He grabs my hands and pushes them to my sides, digging his fingers into the skin on my thighs.

"Yet you sought the attention of others. The *touch* of others. Did it feel good when they laid their hands on you? Hmm?"

I shake my head. A tear falls from my lashes.

"Was it thrilling when they talked about *fucking you*?"

I shake my head again. Breathing becomes extremely difficult.

"Do you think you need to be punished, Red?"

I pause, looking over at the two queen beds.

River is straddling Pierce, having already tied him up, fully clothed. Hands to the headboard, feet to the footboard.

I clench my thighs together.

"Answer me," Phoenix growls in my ear as he slides his hands up my arms. Placing them on my shoulders, he walks me toward the foot of the empty bed. "Do you deserve to be punished, Red?"

I take a deep breath and relax into him, allowing myself to go to the place where none of my problems matter. Not when I'm submitting to him. I nod once, knowing that's all he needs.

"Three taps, anywhere, and this all stops. Understand?" I nod, but he reaches around with one arm and grips my chin, holding me in place. "Show me, Raven."

I lift one hand and tap his forearm three times, then drop my hand back to my side.

"Good girl." He chuckles darkly, and my pussy clenches around nothing. The ache this man leaves me in daily should be illegal. "Now, lift your dress above your ass and bend over the end of the fucking bed."

I try my damnedest to hold back the smile on my face, but by River's chuckle, I have a sense that I fail miserably.

"Being extra naughty tonight, Red?" Phoenix asks from behind me.

I shrug as I slide my dress up to show off my very obvious lack of underwear, then rest my forearms on the mattress. My deep red curls provide a curtain around my rapidly heating face, and I let my smile slip.

"Raven," Phoenix says as he slides his palms up my ankles and the back of my thighs. "I want you to listen closely. You put yourself in danger tonight. By doing that, you also put *us* in danger. We could have ended up in prison or dead instead of right here with you."

The lack of warmth in his tone is the only warning I get before his hand slaps down onto my bare ass. I shift forward, stuff my face into the mattress, and let out a long breath.

"We'd do anything for you, and you took advantage of that."

Smack!

"While being told your punishment, you little minx, you fucking *smiled.*"

Smack!

"And you went out *without panties!*"

Smack!

He groans as he runs a finger through my folds, and I listen intently to the sounds I hope are him cleaning my juices from his fingers.

"And to top it all off... you're fucking *wet* for it."

"How wet?" River asks. He's breathless, as if he's already stroking himself.

I want to see what he's doing, but I'm too busy drooling onto the mattress to lift my head.

Phoenix's palm makes contact one last time, right at the juncture of my thighs, and he leaves his hand there to soak up the heat from his sting as I writhe underneath him. He chuckles when I try to move up the bed, then uses his free hand to push down between my shoulder blades. "She's fucking soaking."

"Fuck," River breathes, and I twist my head enough to

see him. He's sitting next to Pierce, naked, with his hand fisting his dick. "Hey little vixen," he says when he meets my gaze.

I dart my eyes to Pierce and back, inquiring if he's okay. I haven't heard a single thing from him.

"Passed out. He'll be fine." River grunts as he twists his hand over his head, then stands from the bed and walks over to us. "Can I join in over here?" He places his hand on my cheek and brushes a hair away with his thumb.

I eagerly nod just as Phoenix thrusts two fingers inside of me, stealing my breath as my mouth gapes open.

"Perfect timing, Nixy," River says, stuffing his dick between my parted lips.

"Take us both to Hell and back, Red, and I'll let you come." Phoenix leans down to place a kiss on my shoulder blade before removing his fingers and replacing them with the head of his cock.

"Oh shit," River grunts, placing his hand on the back of my skull. "Feels so good, little vixen."

Tears fall from my lashes. Of exhaustion, arousal, from not being able to breathe with River's dick so far down my throat. It's euphoric being used like this, but also being the one with the power to start and stop it at will.

They bow to me while tossing me on my knees, and I fucking love it.

"So wet." Phoenix groans. "Fuck, Red. You're going to be the end of us." He slaps my ass a few times, moaning when I buck against him. "I'll spank you whenever you want, baby." He chuckles and thrusts into me harder.

I hollow my cheeks out for River, reaching a hand up to roll his balls in one of my hands.

"Shit," he stutters, nostrils flaring as his eyes widen.

"Just like that, sweet vixen." He huffs out a breath. "I'm gonna fucking come," he shouts before he spurts down my throat.

I swallow it all like the good girl I never try to be, then take a much needed deep breath. Only I lose the ability to breathe again when Phoenix reaches around to rub my clit, grinding himself inside of me until he's stimulating everything all at once.

River leans down to kiss me, running his hands over my breasts and tweaking my nipples.

"Come for us, Red." Phoenix demands. He pinches my clit and sends me soaring.

I don't know what happens next, only that someone carries me, and I start to cry.

A lot.

It's as if the world itself has crumpled around me and all the dumb decisions I've ever made are coming back to haunt me.

"I've got her," Phoenix whispers. "Take care of him if he wakes up."

"Alright," River replies. He looks down at me with a mixture of worry and love on his face. "Have a good bath, RaeRae. You'll be okay."

I sniffle and nod, leaning my head back into Phoenix as another silent sob wracks my body.

"The adrenaline wore off, Red. You'll be fine. You're safe," Phoenix says. "I've got you."

CHAPTER TEN

"Thanks man," I say, giving the guy from room service a hundred dollar tip before closing the door and sliding the lock back into place.

His job was on the line the second he passed over four Bloody Marys to an underage college student, so I'm going to pay it forward in case he needs to find a new profession. I set the tray down on the table in the corner before I slide the balcony curtains wide open. My lips stretch into a wide grin when Pierce hisses like a cat. Fucking pansy ass. Never does take a hangover well.

I've yet to really see Red with a bad one, but I'm suspecting I might be lucky this morning.

"What the fuck, Nix?" Pierce snaps, sitting up and rubbing at his wrists where River had wrapped them up last night.

"Nasty rope burns, Jackson." I walk over to him and give him a drink. A peace offering.

"Can't believe I fell asleep after he tied me up, too." He

takes a sip, pulls a pickle off a stick, and bites into it. "What the hell happened last night?"

"You mean before or after Nix made Rae fuck you with a strap-on?" River asks, sleep unmistakable in his groggy voice.

Pierce splutters liquid and bits of pickle out of his mouth, turning his head to glare at River, then me. "No, she... tell me... wait... really?"

Can't figure out if the idea intrigues him or not.

I bark out a quick laugh, wincing when the sound echoes and glance down at a still heavily sleeping Raven. The two idiots on the other bed are staring at me as I kiss her cheek. "No, dumbass. Your ass hurt?"

He shakes his head, his mouth already full of food and drink again.

"It should be obvious. I'd have her use a bigger one than what Jacobs is packing, that's for sure." I chuckle as I walk to get River his Bloody Mary. After I deliver it, nodding at his mumbled thanks, I grab another for Raven and sit down next to her, placing my free hand in her hair.

"She'll never wake up at this point," Pierce states after, thankfully, swallowing his food. "She used to sleep this hard after an all-nighter and I couldn't wake her up until the late afternoon, sometimes not even then."

"Well," River says with a groan as he sits up. "We have to get cleaned up and leave in a bit. What's our next stop, Nixy-boy?"

"New Mexico."

"Do we have to camp out there?" Pierce asks. "We could find a small hotel on our way and—"

"I want to camp," River says. "Rae wants to camp. We outvoted you, PJ."

"Nix never voted, so that's bullshit."

"I want to camp, too," I tell him, looking up to meet his gaze. "It's supposed to be nice out there at night, too. It'll be a great detox from the city."

Raven's hand meets my side and trails upwards, and I blow out a breath as goosebumps follow in her wake. She smiles when I shiver and I move the hair that's fallen in front of her eyes to see them wide open and staring directly up at me.

"Good morning, beautiful," I tell her, loving how her eyes widen a fraction at the compliment. "I have a hangover cure for you. Drink it all. We have to shower and head out."

She nods and yawns, sitting up slowly as she reaches for the glass. Her eyelids close a few times as she takes a sip, but she starts to nibble on the food as she downs it.

I lean over and kiss her temple before standing and grabbing my own drink. "I'll be back," I tell them as I exit the room onto the balcony.

RYAN

Hey man, give me a call ASAP. Got news on Lexi's case you might want information on.

I sit down heavily in one of the chairs and dial his number and sip from my drink. The Strip is empty this morning. Not completely void of people, but still different from last night.

"Hey, Nix," Ryan answers. "Give me a second, babe. I'll be right back."

"But we just got on the phone, Ry!" I tease him, and he chuckles.

"You bozo," he retorts.

I relax as a door closes in the background and I grab a pickle from my drink.

"Whitaker is out for blood on this one."

I sit up straighter to avoid choking on the pickle currently trying to lodge its way down my throat. "What?"

"There's supposed to be a trial starting for Xavier Hayes real soon. I don't think it'll even make it *that far*, though. Whitaker's been spewing shit to anyone who will listen about how he can get Xavier to fess up to his crimes."

"But Xavier didn't—" I clear my throat and try again. "How does he know Xavier did it?"

Ryan scoffs. "If Whitaker Sommers says someone did something, they did it, so it doesn't matter. Not really. You realize this more than anyone, Nix."

I groan and close my eyes, but open them when I see visions of being locked up in a police station for hours while Whitaker tried to pin the blame on me for something Lexi did. It was just a graffitied wall, but I had a clean reputation I wanted to keep. Lexi was *not* happy that I told the truth about her doing it and didn't talk to me for three weeks.

"What I don't understand is," Ryan says, "if that was my kid, my daughter, right? I'd want to find out the truth about what happened."

"What if she actually did this herself?" I ask.

"It'd piss me the fuck off, but I wouldn't make shit up, like Whitaker is doing. Do you think she committed suicide, Nix?"

"Not in a traditional sense, no. This was a long game for her. Too many wrong decisions lumped together." I sigh and rest my head back against the chair, staring up at the slats of the balcony above us.

"I'm sorry, man." After a pause, he lets out a slow breath

and I mimic it in an attempt to calm my racing thoughts. "You gonna be okay? I get you're on this like... trip with your crew or whatever, but if you need anything..."

"I'll be fine. You know, lost in the hows and whys. How do we get from one place to another? That type of shit." I take a long pull from my drink, then put the glass on the table. "I'm gonna go back to my girl now, Ry. Keep me updated, okay?"

"They set the trial to start next week, but if I find out anything before that, I'll call or text. Rachel wants to be a news reporter, and she's interning right now." He chuckles. "She's obsessed with this case, so I probably hear more than I legally should."

I swear, one of these days, those two need to stop ignoring their attraction for each other.

Whether Max the Manwhore is involved in that or not...

No one can predict the future of that inevitable shit show.

"Well, tell her good luck from me. I'll come see you guys over the summer. For a show or two."

"Hey, if Phoenix West is coming back into town, we're gonna get your ass up on stage. You realize that, right?"

I bark out a laugh. "Okay, Ry. Go right the fuck ahead if you think you can. Stay sane, brother."

"You know that's a hard one, Nix, but you, too."

After hanging up with him, I drink the rest of my Bloody Mary before standing and walking back inside.

Everyone showered, and they're sitting on the bed playing a card game together. Rae's dressed in too short shorts and a crop top that struggles to cover the bottom of her bra, and Pierce and River are both wearing khaki shorts and shirts from a music tour they went to over the summer.

I pass by them all to take a shower. Once I'm done, we pack up, check out, and take off for New Mexico.

Leaving Vegas is strange. While we were here for only one night, it put things into perspective for us.

River was allowed to flaunt his relationship with Pierce freely out here, and Pierce just let him, no questions asked.

Pierce learned the hard way that our girl is *not* a fucking object, though it's a lesson we'll continue beating into him if he needs to keep being told.

Raven got a glimpse of what it's like when we're all at her beck and fucking call, even when she isn't the one calling for us in times of crisis. We feel it in our souls when she needs us.

I'm having a hard time coming to terms with a few things, but I've learned something extremely important through this one small spring break pit stop, and that's that I am one million fucking percent in love with Raven Hill.

And it scares me more than I'd like to admit.

Is he okay?

RIV

Yeah, baby, he's okay.

I feel like such an asshole, Riv.

RIV

Nope. Don't do that. He's crossed too
many of your boundaries, Rae. Too many of
mine and Nix's too, to be honest. You did
good telling him off.

It just feels... wrong, somehow.

RIV

That's because you've never had to set
them with him before. Nix and I back this
decision 100%. Don't worry, okay?

Just... help him through this. Somehow.

RIV

I've got a few ideas up my sleeve.
Seriously. Don't worry.

What if he never changes?

What if he's always like this to me?

I seriously can't think of a world without me
and him together, but I can't let him abuse
me like that anymore, either.

RIV

If he has to stand by and never touch you
for the rest of his life... he'll do it. He loves
you, he just needs to learn what the word
consent fucking means.

I hope you're right. I already miss him.

raven

"Hey, hey, hey wait!" River shouts, pointing toward yet another billboard. "It's 'The Great Mysterio'." He holds his arms out and wiggles his fingers as if he's doing magic, his gray eyes wide with mischief.

I snort a laugh and grab a chip from the bag Phoenix is holding, then stuff it in my mouth as I glance out the window.

"Alright, alright," Pierce says, shoving River away by the head. "I spy... something black."

River and I search around the car before staring at Pierce in annoyance. The interior of the entire vehicle is black.

"Raven's bra strap," Phoenix states from my side, reaching over to pluck it from my skin.

It snaps against my shoulder and I playfully swat him as I rub my hand over the sore spot.

"How the fuck was I supposed to see that from up here, Pierce?" River sighs and tosses his head back. He turns it to look at me. "Stop smiling! It's just encouraging his bullshit."

"Sorry to break the news," Pierce says as he slides his sunglasses on his face. "She's been supporting my bullshit since we were eight years old."

"Don't use the home field advantage!" River folds his arms and glares between us before putting his own sunglasses on. He reaches forward to turn the music back up a little.

I lift my legs up onto the seat and rest them in Phoenix's lap, grateful when he takes my feet and massages them.

Being in the car this long has its advantages and disadvantages, but mostly it's just been good for us to be locked away like this. No one's around to bother us, and we've gotten to watch the world as we pass it by. Tonight will be more fun because we'll be camping.

Pierce and I used to do this every weekend at our park at home.

"How much further?" River asks.

"If I knew the name of the campground, this would be easier," Pierce says.

"I told you, it doesn't have one." River spins in his seat and hands me a package of peanut butter cups, which I take with a grateful smile and immediately open. "Besides," he says as he turns back around, opening his own, "the pin I put on the map will lead you directly to our spot for the night. Promise."

Pierce sighs and runs a hand through his hair, and I reach toward him, resting my palm on his shoulder. His head lifts and his lips lift into a grateful smile before he twists our fingers together. "It claims we should be there in about an hour. Just in time for dinner."

"Great," River says cheerfully. "That's enough time for another nap!"

"YOU'VE GOT to be fucking kidding me," Pierce says as he stops in front of a wide expanse of dirt.

And dirt.

And more dirt.

"This isn't a fucking campground, Jacobs," Phoenix snaps as he slaps a hand on the other's shoulder.

"It is if we're camping on it." River spreads his arms and spins as if to show us all the beauty of the place.

I have to admit, the emptiness of the land has its own charm. The red dirt, a few cacti here and there. Tumbleweeds. I have to keep from scratching my exposed skin. But we're alone out here, not cramped around other campers, and kept to the rules of a normal campsite.

"At what point do you plan to quit lying to get your way, Riv?" Pierce asks as he tosses down the bag with our tent. The metal poles clang together as it lands.

River shrugs and winks before tossing a few of our bags onto the ground. "Good thing I said we should stop at that last gas station and grab some stuff for a fire, huh?"

"River," Phoenix sighs, rubbing the bridge of his nose. "The fucking bathroom is a five-minute walk away!"

I step in front of River and place my hands on either side of his face with the express intention to get him to change his mind, but then I sigh when he looks down at me with hope in his eyes. I shake my head as I pull away, then sign, *Where do we put the tent up?*

"Yes!" he shouts, raising his fist in the air before looking around. "Over there works. I'll get the fire started, and we may have to dig a hole somewhere for Rae to pee in. It'll be fine, guys. My father and I used to go camping all the time. I've got this!"

"What, were you a boy scout?" Pierce mocks as he drags our gear where River tells him to.

"Nope. Didn't want to be because of the rules. Plus, my dad wanted to lead a troop. That would have ended badly for everyone." River helps Pierce take out the tent, and I sit my happy ass down on one of the boys' bags.

Phoenix joins them, and for the next thirty minutes I watch three grown ass men struggle to do a task that would have been easier if they'd just read the fucking directions.

I should have saved my popcorn.

"I'm going to shove this pole up your ass, River Jacobs." Pierce sighs and tosses it to the ground. "I thought you knew what the fuck you were doing."

"It's been a minute," River says, grunting when he gets a pole in place. "Now we just have to anchor the bottoms and put the rain fly on."

"Do you plan for it to rain tonight?" Pierce snaps, glaring daggers at River.

River shrugs and points toward a bag at my feet. "Hey Rae, can you bring me the mallet and stakes, please?"

I grab what he wants and swing the mallet around in my hand as I approach them. I'd taken my shoes off a while ago, and the sand is quickly cooling as evening approaches. It's soothing between my toes, and reminds me of my childhood.

"Careful, you've pissed her off enough to swing a hammer in your direction, Jacobs." Phoenix grins at River, tying the last piece to the tent before taking a step and folding his arms over his chest.

"Don't hurt me, Rae," River says in a plea. "I promise I'll pick an oasis to camp at next time."

I raise a brow and shake my head, huffing out a quick laugh before handing him the bag. If they want to work against the hard soil beneath them to get those stakes in, I'll let them have at it.

I turn around and walk toward our bags, grabbing a snack pack out of it as I wait for them to finish setting up.

"You still up for a little hike in the morning, Red?" Phoenix crouches down next to me and snags a cracker out of my hand before popping it into his own mouth.

I take a sip of my water and nod.

"If we make it to the top, River said it has a great view. Might have to get up super early to beat the heat."

You act like I didn't spend most of my summers getting Pierce up at the ass crack of dawn to run around outside, I sign. I laugh when River tosses the last stake at Pierce, missing his head by barely an inch.

"They're both idiots." Phoenix wraps an arm around my shoulders and I sigh, resting against him.

They're my idiots, I sign.

"I CAN'T BELIEVE you thought the hard ass ground here would take those stakes that easily, Jacobs!" Pierce shouts across the fire, laughing when River narrows his eyes.

"Are you going to keep doing that? We're just gonna keep talking about it? Beat the dead horse into the ground?" River sighs as he sits next to me, pulling me into his lap as he hands me the wine cooler I asked for. "Take your grown up juice and protect me from the grump, please."

I shake my head, silently giggling as I sip from the bottle, my eyes locked on Pierce's across the fire.

With bellies full of hot dogs and chips, we've settled on enjoying each other's company until we have to leave at lunch tomorrow.

We'd planned this trip to be an actual vacation, not just a mission to get Mark Riley on our side, so we spent a while picking destinations and deciding when to stop. Especially since Pierce refuses to allow anyone else to drive. River, unfortunately, got to pick this one. He just wanted to go camping with us all. Reprogram his brain so he'd remember our trip over the ones with his father.

"You smell like campfire and booze, little vixen," River whispers in my ear.

I shiver and sip from my drink again, resting my back against his chest.

"Hey, it's not late enough for all that," Pierce complains.

"Calm down, big guy," Phoenix says. "I've got the s'mores supplies."

"Fuck yes!" River shouts, startling me. Some of my drink spills, and I wince. "Shit. Sorry." He tilts my chin and licks the alcohol up before capturing my lips in a too-quick kiss.

I look back at the other two, breathless. Their eyes lock on us as they open the packages. I bite my lip to hold back my grin and turn my gaze to the fire and watch a piece of wood as it breaks off after having burned for over an hour.

"We gonna use real sticks?" Pierce asks.

I glance up and sign, *If we use the metal things, I'm disowning you all.*

"The metal things are cleaner," Phoenix says.

"They're also cheating us out of the full experience," Pierce replies as he stands and passes out sticks. He'd already prepared the ends with his pocket knife, and I thank him with a soft kiss before holding my hand out for a marshmallow from Phoenix.

"You guys are heathens," he complains, but he still hands me a marshmallow.

We roast them in companionable silence, watching as they either melt or burn until we have to pull them out of the fire or sacrifice them to the flames.

Soft music plays from someone's phone off to the side, and I twist my hips a little while I put my s'more together. I grin when I take a bite, tossing my head back and staring at the clear night sky while the mix of flavors explodes in my mouth.

The boys chatter about life, but I don't listen.

I let myself go for a while, to feel young and free and not like *me* for just long enough to experience a full breath for the first time in a while. The light from the fire and stars guide me as I dance barefoot in the middle of the desert. A deeper bass hums in the air and one of my boys comes up behind me. His hands trail from my thighs to my hips before directing my movements, and he grips me tight to his front.

Pierce.

He wraps his arm around my front as the bass drops again and collars my throat, pulling my back against him as he lifts my head and trails kisses along my skin until he reaches my ear.

"What are you doing, little bird?" The smell of beer and chocolate on his breath relaxes me.

I grind my ass against his erection as the beat continues

to throb through me, and he groans. Wetness pools between my thighs and I squirm in his hold.

"Strip for us, Blue." He moves back and swats my ass as he goes.

I turn to see him adjusting himself before he sits down on the ground next to the other two, who are staring at me with lust shining in their eyes. Swallowing, I summon my inner succubus and lift my hands up my body, dragging my fingers along my skin, my shorts, my stomach, until I cup my own breasts over my crop top, twisting myself this way and that.

If it's a show they want, it's a show they'll get.

This version of me loves the attention.

I bite my lip as I move my shirt over my head, and I listen intently to their reactions. How they swallow, stop breathing, shift on the ground. I let loose a feral grin as I lower my hands to my shorts and turn, shaking my ass for them as I slide them down my legs. Looking over my shoulder, I toss a wink at them before standing and moving my body to the beat again, my fingers buried in my hair.

"Fuck," River whispers, and my grin spreads.

I reach around and unsnap my bra, sliding it off both of my arms before tossing it behind me, shoulders shaking with my laugh when one grunts as if he got hit by it. Turning my head, I slowly slide my underwear down until they're at my feet. I step out of them and hold them in the air as I turn, staring down at my men before tossing the underwear directly at Pierce. Intending to be the tease that I want to be tonight, I turn toward the tent and take off like a rocket, pretending my squeal echoes in the night as all three of them bolt to their feet and chase after me.

It's not far, only a few feet, but I struggle to get the

zipper to open and they're on me within milliseconds. We land in a pile of limbs on top of our sleeping bags.

I grip Pierce's biceps tight as he leans over me, sliding us further into the tent until he's leaning his whole body over my naked one, my legs on either side of his hips. My breathing is coming out in pants as I stare into his eyes, licking my lips as I wait for his next move.

"You're fucking perfect," he whispers before descending on me, his lips pressing firm to mine and stealing my breath.

"Don't steal her all to yourself," Phoenix says, grabbing my jaw and turning my head until he can kiss me, forcing Pierce to back away.

River leans in and kisses Pierce just as Phoenix devours me whole, and I clench my thighs together around Pierce's torso, grinding against him.

Pierce groans and moves his hand between us, rubbing light circles around my clit as he continues to make out with River, and Phoenix bites my lower lip, sucking it into his mouth.

I'm overwhelmed by their touch, and it's more intoxicating than any drink I've ever had.

"Fuck, you're so wet," Pierce says as he pulls away from River.

Phoenix finally lets me go, kissing my neck and shoulder as he trails his hands up and down my sides.

I grind against Pierce's hand, my eyes locked on his again as he thrusts two fingers inside me.

"Gonna let me fuck this sweet pussy, little bird? Make you feel good?" Pierce adds another finger, and I nod because I'd do anything to have him inside me right now.

River sits up on his haunches and reaches into his bag, then pulls out a bottle of lube, staring pointedly at Pierce.

Pierce's entire body shudders before he nods at River and leans down to kiss me again. His lips are warm against mine, and I tangle my fingers in his hair as we lay there, making out like normal teenagers. We forget everything else for so long, Phoenix intervenes with a tug of my hair.

"What am I going to do with you, Red?" Phoenix asks, eyes sparkling with a dark promise just before he leans down and kisses me possessively.

Pierce grunts, and my mind goes wild, imagining River thrusting inside of him.

I open my eyes to see River just above Pierce's shoulder, and I break away from my kiss with Phoenix just as Pierce notches his dick at my entrance. Our eyes stay locked as Pierce enters me, and the moment feels significant. As if the three of us joined like this cements something in my heart.

Phoenix turns my head again, and I lick my lips when he pops my jaw open, nudging his dick inside. "Good girl," he praises, and I clench around Pierce.

"Shit," River says, laughing. "This is some magic chain reaction shit going on."

"What?" Pierce asks. He groans when River thrusts forward, and my eyes shut when that pushes him further into me, then Phoenix groans when that closes my mouth tighter around him.

Phoenix lets out a slight laugh and tosses his head back. He thrusts into my mouth at a slow and steady pace, shifting my body so it slides along Pierce's shaft.

I'm sure if we were to get caught out in a random desert in this position, we'd all go to jail for public debauchery, and not a single one of us would feel guilty for it.

I let out a breath through my nose when Phoenix thrusts further, holding my head in place.

Pierce wraps his arms around me until he can anchor his hands on my shoulders, pulling me down onto him as he thrusts inside. He hits the perfect spot that has me quivering, spasming, on the verge of combusting.

"Play with her clit," Phoenix directs, his jaw locked tight as he holds himself back.

Pierce moves, but River beats him to it. He slides his hand between our bodies and grinds his palm against my clit in circles as he continues to thrust into Pierce.

"Come for us, little vixen," he commands as he adds more pressure.

Pierce grinds his cock inside of me at such an angle that I detonate, seeing the stars far beyond the ones we can see outside. White floods my vision, and my body seizes between my men, fingers clutching wherever I can get them, toes curling into Pierce's thighs, mouth tightening around Phoenix's dick. I can't breathe, much less think, and I don't have the energy to be embarrassed when one of them says I squirted.

Phoenix comes down my throat a moment later, and the others follow shortly after, both letting out heavy breaths as they lean as little of their body weight on me as possible.

"You okay?" Phoenix whispers in my ear before kissing my cheek.

I nod and close my eyes while my lips tilt up into a lazy smile.

"I'm dead," Pierce says.

"Too soon, Jackson," River says, kissing Pierce's cheek, then mine. He pulls out of Pierce and sits on top of his own sleeping bag, catching his breath.

"I love you," Pierce whispers to me before kissing my lips and pulling out.

I wince at the mess we've all made, but I'm not messy for long.

Phoenix plucks out a container of wipes and the boys take a few minutes to clean me up before wrapping me in a fresh blanket and tucking me between them all.

I guess camping doesn't always have to be boring.

river

"You're a teenager now, River. You need to start bringing more kids in for the Youth Group." My father's voice is grating against my ears, but I nod at his request. Anything to make him happy.

Anything to make him shut the fuck up.

"Thirteen," he says, placing an arm around my shoulders. "I can't believe you're thirteen. You're growing up so fast, son."

I shrug, because he always says weird shit like this and I never know what to say back. I never want to say anything back, but sometimes he makes me.

"How's your reading going?"

I step over a log and curse inside my head when I stumble. He hates when I fuck up in any capacity, even accidentally. "Good. I'm almost finished with Matthew."

"It's taken you almost a year, River. I expected you to be done by now."

I chew the inside of my lip. "I know, sir. I'm sorry, sir."

He pats me on the back hard enough to force me forward a few steps, then passes me a water bottle. "Here."

"Thank you, sir." I open the cap and take a large sip, grateful when we stop at the end of the trail, looking over the town below us. It's not much, our little town, but it's still home. I can see the church in the distance, and I pretend I'm running from it, leaving it behind.

"I have a few more lessons for you today, son. So why don't you put down the water bottle and—"

I WAKE, screaming, sweating, swatting off all the hands that try to hold me down. I shake my head as I shuffle out of the tent and don't even make it a foot away before I throw up everywhere. After a few minutes, when nothing else comes out, I sit on my ass in the dirt and let out an unintelligible scream.

"River," a voice says from beside me.

I glance over to meet Pierce's concerned gaze, but wave him off as I snatch the water bottle from his hand. If only he knew the irony of the gesture. I chug half of it before dangling it between my knees and staring up at the sky.

"I'm fine." I lie.

I'm not.

I'm never fine when I have these fucking nightmares, and the more we talk about trafficking, the more we bring my father up, the more they come around. Escaping him is not an option. I hide a lot of my shit well by either not sleeping or exhausting myself until my body crashes, but I wasn't tired enough today. I wasn't able to work out my frustrations until my energy was depleted.

Pierce climbs back into the tent, leaving me to my

thoughts. But that won't do, so I follow him and curl up in the space he's left between him and Rae.

Those pretty blues stare at me as best she can in the darkness, and I rest my forehead against hers and breathe her in.

"Rest, Rae," I whisper. "I'll be okay."

She dozes after a while, as does Pierce, but I stay awake to watch my crew sleep, warding off the flashbacks until my eyes burn and I have no choice but to close them.

"PHOENIX," I groan. "The sun isn't even up."

"That's the point of a sunrise hike," he says, passing a water bottle to me.

I wish I was allergic to the things so no one could ever give me one again, but since I'm not, I stuff the bottle in my back pocket and wrap an arm around a yawning Rae. "Ready to go for a hike for Mr. Sadistic?"

She leans into me, clutching her own bottle between her hands as she shrugs.

Phoenix leads us toward this trail he found on an app, and I'll be the first to admit it's got a cool vibe in the morning. The sun won't rise until we're at the top, not fully, so there's a blue glow over every surface we see, as though the world is stuck in time.

I yawn, and Rae wraps her arm around me as we walk along a flat trail. I look down at her and see the concern I wish I could avoid. "You want to know about it, don't you?" She nods and I groan, tossing my head back.

"It'd be easier if you just opened up," Pierce says from behind us, and I flip him off over my head.

Phoenix is walking a few feet ahead, earbuds in as he listens to music. He's the first to wake in the mornings, and when it's warm out, he'll go for walks or runs, depending on his mood. He's responsible, whereas I am the complete opposite.

I'd rather stay in bed and get as much sleep as possible.

"Okay, so I've told you my dad was an abusive dick. He's the pastor of the church, yada, yada." I help Rae up a steep step, then wrap my arm around her shoulders again. "Well, he used to bring me out on camping trips a lot. He'd say they were father and son bonding times, and those were when he'd abuse me the most. The longer we were alone, the worse it got for me. Sometimes they were just simple chats about life, as if he wanted me to get used to being alone with him like that, away from the world, but then he'd start screaming about shit sometimes." I laugh and run my free hand through my hair. "It was stupid shit. He'd expect me to do things I couldn't possibly do, and there was one time when he and my mom got into a fight." I swallow hard before taking a deep breath.

Rae hugs me close, kissing my chest as she waits for me to continue.

"He kicked me out of the house after their fight, saying it was all my fault and that if they ever got a divorce, he'd come after me. Like." I pause and bark out a loud laugh. "Like if they fight and divorce, it's absolutely my fault and not theirs, right?" I shake my head and take a few deep breaths to calm myself. "On top of it all, though, these camping trips he'd take me on were for him to abuse me. Sexually."

"Fuck man," Pierce whispers. "You never said—"

"You never fucking asked, PJ," I snap, turning my head to glare at him.

He winces. "I'm a selfish prick, okay? I'm sorry."

Shrugging, I look forward again to avoid tripping over anything. "I never told anyone, and I never planned to, honestly. It was easier to keep it to myself than be told I was a liar."

"Your dad's a lot like Whitaker Sommers, right?" Phoenix asks. He's sitting on a log and taking a drink of water.

I shrug. "I don't know about Whitaker, but it's possible."

"Whitaker owns his town. Everyone listens to him. He's the be all, end all." Phoenix scoffs and shakes his head, letting it hang between his shoulders for a moment.

"I guess so. I feel like my dad doesn't have as much pull, but if he's friends with Maxwell and Whitaker, then I don't see it being too far of a stretch."

Rae sits next to Phoenix on the log and takes a sip from her water bottle before putting it between her legs. *Do you guys really think they're all working together?* She signs.

"They've gotta be," Pierce says.

"It would make the most logical sense. They've been friends for so long." Phoenix stands and helps Rae up.

"What do we do about them?" I ask, because there's not a fucking chance we're letting this shit slide anymore. Not with them targeting Rae.

"One step at a time, River," Phoenix says, patting my shoulder as he passes. "Come on. Up we go. We're almost there."

I toss my head back and groan as I follow them up the

last stretch. Not hard to do with Rae's ass cheeks hanging out of her shorts like that.

"You gonna be okay, Riv?" Pierce asks as we take the last few steps up the hill.

I shrug and let out a deep breath when we crest the top. I'm unable to respond when I see the view before us.

The sun is rising behind the trees, the orange glow is bright against the dark blues and greens. The pink and reds set the sky ablaze, and there, just in front of me, stands Raven with her deep red curls and gorgeous body.

She turns, a bright smile on her face as she looks back to all of us, and my heart threatens to stop beating in my chest with how much love I feel for this girl.

"Yeah," I tell Pierce finally. "I'm gonna be okay."

RAERAE

What the hell are you doing over there?

You can only find out if you promise to keep a secret from the grump.

RAERAE

gif of a girl zipping lips

There's a place that sells jewelry made with jizz.

Jizzy Jewelry.

RAERAE

shocked face emoji

I'm trying not to laugh at this place. I'm being an adult about it. Mostly.

RAERAE

Wait... so why aren't we telling Pierce about it?

I'm gonna have them make him a bracelet. I'm paying extra to get it done tonight.

RAERAE

So wait... you're gonna give them YOUR jizz?

Abso-fuckin-lutely babe.

And you won't tell him, and neither will I.

RAERAE

So... he'll wear it and never know it's made of jizz?

line of laughing emojis

Careful, he's trying to look over your shoulder. Kick him in the shin or something.

RAERAE

Will we ever tell him?

Nah. I'm taking this shit to my grave.

raven

I told him once that I was going to run him over with his own car if he kept micromanaging the way I drove, I sign to River before reaching forward and snagging another Red Vine. When he glares at me, I chew it off defiantly and wink at him in the mirror.

"I can't read what you're saying back there, but I know it's bullshit. She telling lies, Riv?" He reaches into a bag and grabs a chip, throwing it behind him.

It hits me in the head and I laugh before tossing it back at him, grinning when he flips me off.

"She just said she's glad she has us now, because we eat her pussy better." River laughs when I lean toward him and shove him in the shoulder, pushing him into the window.

Phoenix looks down at his phone, a frown growing on his face once again.

I chew my lower lip before leaning forward and planting a kiss on his cheek, sighing when all I get in return is a small smile before he turns back to it. I wish he'd tell me more of what's going on, but he's keeping to himself more and more as the hours continue to drag on.

"Hey, Nixy-boy," River calls as he leans between the front seats. "You gonna get out of your head, or just stay there for the rest of the trip? It's a *lot* of work entertaining these two."

"Not much to do in the car, River," Phoenix says, sighing when River kisses his cheek. "Please sit back down. We have a long night in this car and I'd hate to kill you and have your rotting flesh stink up the place for the next twelve hours."

"Dramatic, much?" River grumbles as he sits back down, handing me another Red Vine.

I take a bite and glance out my window, simply watching the night sky as we fly down the road. I perk up when I see a strange glow in the distance, patting Pierce on the shoulder to point it out to him.

"We have a long night ahead of us, Blue. I can't make another detour..." He sighs when our gaze meets in the rearview and I give him a pleading look. Rolling his eyes, he slows until he can get off the next exit. "Fine. It's probably something dumb, though."

"A fucking abandoned race track is far from dumb," River says ten minutes later when we're all standing inside of a speedway littered with people and cars.

So. Many. Cars.

My gaze latches onto a purple Mustang before Pierce gets into my field of vision, grabbing my cheeks and pulling my face up to his.

His eyes are wild with the boyish excitement I love from him, and adrenaline fills his kiss. "Nice fucking catch, babe."

I shrug and wrap my arm around his waist as we walk toward the bleachers where the guys plant us in the front row, closest to the barriers, in order to see better. My knee is bouncing like crazy, the thought of getting inside one of the cars consuming my thoughts, but Pierce grips my thigh and leans over to kiss my cheek.

"Bucket list item?" he asks, and I nod. "Hey, Riv!"

"What's up?" River asks.

"Let's go see if we can get in a couple of those cars." Pierce stands and wraps an arm around River's shoulders, walking away from me, but not before he tosses a wink over his shoulder.

"What's that all about?" Phoenix asks as he slides into the vacant spot on my left.

Pierce and I used to talk about bucket list items a lot. One of his was to race. Mine was to do a ride along, I sign, then shrug.

Phoenix places his phone in his pocket, and my heart jolts inside of my chest when he pulls me to sit on his lap. "Does the racing get your blood flowing, Red?"

I rest my back against his front and nod, wrapping my hands over his forearms when he wraps them around my waist.

Pierce and River climb into two separate cars down the line a bit, and I watch with anticipation thrumming through my veins as they snag helmets and listen to the rundown on the vehicles.

The cars set to race before my guys—A black Camaro and Firebird—slide up to the starting line as a girl walks up to stand between them. She waves a flag this way, holds it high above her head, then drops it with a shout which is drowned out by the loud roar of the car engines, and the smell of burnt rubber intensifies as both cars take off, smoke billowing from behind them.

I squirm in Phoenix's lap, imagining what the adrenaline must be like from inside one of those cars. The intense speed, the way your body would push back against the seat, unable to do anything but hang out and hope you beat your opponent. Losing control would be cathartic.

Phoenix slides a palm across my ribs, down my stomach, and into the waistband of my shorts. He groans in my ear, and my back arches as I let out a breath. His hand slides further, and he cups me outside of my underwear. "Do you want to be fingered in a race car, Red? Is that your bucket list item?"

I nod frantically, hoping he'll take some of the pressure off.

"Too bad we're not in one, huh?" He pulls his hand from my pants and I twist around to glare at him.

He grins and kisses my lips. "I won't drive one, but the other two are about to, so let's get up close and watch."

I sigh and slide off his lap. We walk toward the barriers and lean against them right at the starting line.

Our boys are next, and damn, they're sexy as they roll up beside one another in those cars.

Pierce sits tall and proud in the purple Mustang, because of course he does, and River's in a baby blue Camaro. He revs the engine a few times when he sees me plastered to the barrier closest to him. He winks and I blow them both a kiss.

For a moment, I breathe in the night air, the burning rubber, the oil, and release it all alongside the tension of our mounting problems.

Fuck Maxwell Langston for ruining what should be the best years of our lives. Revenge is going to be served, and soon.

Phoenix slides up behind me and places his hands on either side of me on top of the barrier, gripping it tightly as he rests his head atop mine. His warmth is comforting when he's been so distant on this trip. Some of my tension falls away in his presence.

"Alright, ladies and gentlemen," the announcer calls. "Some newbies are looking to race. Let's see what they're capable of. Let's hear it for Pierce and River!"

The crowd goes wild, and I wish I could scream for them, but I pretend. I let out the world's loudest silent scream, bouncing up and down for them and grinning when their eyes never leave me. We can all pretend, and maybe one day I'll be able to scream for them—in more ways than one.

My skin heats as Pierce's eyes grow fierce from the driver's seat, and just before the flag girl reaches the spot between his and River's cars, he gets out of his and bounds toward me without a care in the world.

"Ride with me?" he asks. He's out of breath and stands inches in front of me, green eyes so vivid as they lock onto me.

I take a deep breath and nod, a bright smile stretching my lips.

"Bucket list item," he shouts as he pulls me over the barrier, Phoenix helping by pushing my ass up and over. Pierce tosses me over his shoulder and smacks my thighs as the crowd whoops and hollers for us, then slides me down his body before helping me into the passenger seat. He hands me a helmet, presses a firm kiss to my lips, then locks it and my seatbelt in place.

With the door closed, I watch him walk around the car and argue with someone who keeps pointing at me.

Must be against the rules to have a ride along, but Pierce doesn't care.

He walks to the driver's side, flips off the person who argued with him, and looks over at me with a wild look in his eyes.

"You ready to fly, little bird?"

I simply nod at him.

So fucking ready to fly.

pierce

She looks so fucking sinful in her shorts and crop top. She's plastered against the seat in both excitement and fear, and her chest is rising and falling with her rapid breathing.

My cock is straining in my pants, but I don't give a fuck about anything but her.

Locking myself into place, I grip the steering wheel with one hand and the gearshift with the other.

"Touch yourself, Raven," I command her, wishing I could, but knowing we wouldn't survive this if I buried my fingers inside of her cunt. It's a miracle I can focus enough to see half a foot in front of me right now.

She reaches down and undoes the button of her shorts, sliding her fingers over herself.

I groan and inhale deeply through my nose, narrowing my eyes on the track. "Two fingers, baby," I tell her.

She does, and the sounds of her slick cunt make me ache to bury myself between her thighs.

Adrenaline gets us off, and she'd always wanted to fuck

around during a race, having seen it in a movie once. The life or death scenario turns her on as much as it does me, and I have a vested interest in her pleasure, so making this happen is a reward for us both.

A girl walks between River and me, holding the flag. I look over to flip him off, laughing at how angry he looks. He adjusts himself in his shorts and flips me off, glaring in a way I just know I'll pay for later.

Game. Fucking. On.

My gaze shifts back to the flag, and I watch it wave from one side to the other. I clutch the steering wheel tighter when Raven tosses her head back against the seat as she plays with herself.

A drag race isn't long. It's short, meant to test who can go the fastest in a small distance. May the better car win. That's it.

River and I did a few over the summer, so I know he's as good as I am at this shit, and that worries me.

Especially since it'll come back to haunt me if I lose.

"You ready to come, little bird?" I ask her, turning my head a little so I can see her as she works herself to an orgasm.

Her free hand massages one of her breasts and I groan, shifting my own hips in search of release.

"God damn," I breathe before I shift my gaze back to the track. "I want you to come the second these cars take off. Fly with the car, got it?"

I listen to the sounds my girl is making with her wet cunt and inhale a deep breath before the flag drops. As soon as it does, I shift as fast as I fucking can while letting off the brake and slamming my foot down on the gas pedal.

Burning rubber assaults my nostrils, but I don't care if I

ruin this fucker's car. Raven's back arches and her mouth opens in a silent scream I wish the world could hear.

River's car jolts ahead, but I shift one more time, and grin when I see the nitro button. I almost break it in my haste to smash it. The air leaves my lungs. We're pushed further back into our seats and sent flying ahead of him, past the finish line, and a little further down the track than necessary.

The car fell silent as I came to a stop a few seconds later, aside from mine and Raven's heavy breathing. I turn my head to look over at the bright smile on her face, the way her palms splay over her stomach, sticky with her release.

I lean over and take her wrist in my hand, shoving her fingers into my mouth and sucking her sweetness off them. "Fuck," I say, sliding my hands into her hair. "That was sexy as all hell. Come here, taste yourself." I slam my lips against hers, kissing her, claiming her. I'm about to pull her over the console when a loud knocking stops us.

"Hey asshole, I want my car back!"

I laugh into our kiss, then turn to open the window for the guy I borrowed the car from. "Alright, alright. Let me drive it back." I don't wait for the fucker to respond. I roll the window up and drive back to the lot.

Raven's shoulders shake with her laughter, and she continues to laugh while I lift her out of the passenger seat to carry her over to the other two sitting on the sidelines. My smile is bright as we approach them, and I know River is about to lay into me for beating him, but I don't care.

I've got my girl, and that's all that matters right now.

"You fucking cheated, Pierce," River snaps as we walk toward the Jeep.

"How did I cheat? We rock paper scissored for the 'Stang,

and I won it." I waggle my brows at him, and he grabs me by the back of my neck, dragging me to him.

"Not only did you steal our girl for yourself, but you cheated to win, and watching her go off like that distracted me. You're rotten, pup." He shoves my head away.

All I can do is laugh.

It's been a long time since I felt this free. Far too fucking long. Since the summer before senior year. "Hey, Blue?"

Rae looks back at me from where she's walking next to Nix, her hand wrapped around his forearm.

"Remember that time we went to the Lookout? You drove my truck, and I rode the bike?" I bring my lower lip between my teeth as I think back to the moment and watch her cheeks heat with the memory.

"You guys have too much fucking history. Sometimes it isn't fair." River tosses an arm over my shoulders. "Share the story with the rest of the family like a good boy."

I roll my eyes, look at Rae for a split second, and shrug. "She was bitching about wanting to do all these normal couple things, and... well... the Lookout was a normal couple thing in our town..."

"GET *your ass in the truck, Raven." I pull open the door and gesture her inside, but she keeps standing there, looking pretty as hell in her short shorts and tank top, arms folded over her chest, hair whipping in the wind. I fucking love this girl, but she's a stubborn shit, and she plays it up.*

Fucking. Daily.

"You wanna go up there?" I ask, trying to maintain a relaxed

and quiet tone. "You wanna go up to the damn Lookout and fuck like rabbits? Huh?" I ask when she doesn't answer. I raise a brow at her as I take a step forward, and grin when she takes a step back. "You forget you're the little bird, and I'm the big, awful cat looking for his next meal."

"You sound ridiculous." But she's turned the fuck on, so I don't care how stupid I sound.

"I've read your dirty books, babe. I know what you like. You think your little highlights go unnoticed?" I shake my head as I laugh, reaching for her hips so I can pull her into me. She squirms in my hold. I watch, transfixed, as her chest rises and falls rapidly with her breathing. "Get your ass in the truck, Raven."

"It's the middle of the day, Pierce. When I said it, I meant for us to go there at night and—"

I place my finger over her lips and shake my head. "No, love. If you want me to fuck you in public, I want to do it so the entire world can see."

"This is stupid," she mumbles around my finger.

"Get in the truck," I tell her again. I turn her toward the open door and smack her ass to get her going. "I'll follow you on the bike."

God knows I want to place her on the seat and eat her until she screams my name over that fucking cliff.

"YOU CAN'T JUST STOP the story there!" River shouts.

I laugh and reach for Raven, pulling her into me much like I did that day. "Why tell you the story when I can show you exactly what the fuck we did?" I waste no time in pressing my lips to Raven's and lifting her up by her thighs, clutching them tightly in my hands. Her warmth paralyzes my dick for a moment as I push her up against the hood of the Jeep. It's a little tall, but I plaster her body to the cold metal, and her back arches as she watches us with heavy-lidded eyes. It doesn't fucking matter what our surroundings are like. We'll make it work. Always do.

"Take her shorts off." I don't care who the fuck does it, only that someone does.

River rushes forward and pulls them down. Phoenix follows behind to remove her underwear.

She glistens in the moonlight. A reminder that the only thing I regret about that day is that I fucked her while the sun burned us to ashes. Her eyes catch mine, glinting with mischief and arousal.

I adjust my dick, then grunt and climb on top of the Jeep. Placing my hand on her chest, I hold her down as I move my pants down past my ass, far enough to free my aching dick. "I loved watching you come in that car, little bird. Now I want you to come all over ours, got it?"

She nods, breathing as heavy as it was back then, and I grin.

"Fuck, you're gorgeous," I say. "You're so filthy for us. Anyone could see us right fucking now, and they'd know what a little slut you are. You're wet enough it shines out here." I plunge a finger inside of her, stretching her, claiming her, heating her up again.

She squirms beneath me, and River clicks his tongue. He approaches the side of the car, and grabs her leg to spread it wide. He gives a pointed look to Phoenix until he does the same. Her nostrils flare and her eyes widen as she's stretched, and I chuckle low in my throat.

"Little different now, huh, little bird?" I tease her as I add another finger. "You only had one filthy fucker to deal with. Now you have three. If it wasn't so hard to do, I'd have them take turns sticking their dicks down your throat right now." She clenches around my fingers and I shake my head. I turn toward River and hold my hand out to his mouth. When he opens his lips, eyes locked on mine, I stick my fingers inside and groan when he licks every last drop of her from them.

Turning away, he looks down at Rae and winks, massaging her thigh as he continues to hold her leg open.

"Eyes on me, Blue," I tell her. I position my dick at her entrance and coat the tip in her juices. Our eyes lock, and like that night almost two years ago, I slide into her slowly, connecting to her more than physically. The universe created our souls for each other. When I bottom out, I let out a pained groan, lean down, and kiss the living fuck out of her. My knees ache as they press against the metal, but I don't give a fuck. I pull out lazily, then push back in just as slowly. I plaster kisses to her lips, her cheeks, her neck, her chest.

The guys let us have this moment, holding her open for me to devour all by myself, and while it's mostly because I won the stupid drag race, it's like they can feel what me and Rae feel. The perfection of our love calling out into the night. And while we make love in the desert, we tell the universe to get fucked.

A man only has so much control, however, and I pick up my pace, plastering a hand on her throat and staring into her eyes. My hips slam against hers, and her head slides up and down the car. She doesn't care. She grinds against me and clenches around me. I use my free hand to work her clit, and seconds later, she seizes beneath me, her mouth parting in an O, and I come inside her with an animalistic growl. I claim her mouth again with my own, still holding her throat, still lightly massaging her clit as she rides the last waves of her orgasm. When I pull back, her breathing is erratic, but she smiles and mouths *'I love you'* and sometimes, or maybe all the time, her love is enough.

"We've got company. May want to cover your ass, Pierce." River laughs, smacking my bare cheek before releasing his hold on Rae. "Hello, gentlemen. Fine night we're having, yeah?" He walks away, and Nix hands her shorts over before following him, no doubt keeping him from making more trouble for us.

Rae and I straighten our clothes, and I place my feet firmly on the ground before reaching for her. "Hands on my shoulders," I tell her. She rolls her eyes, but slides down the hood and does as I ask. I pull her into me as I help her off and kiss her before releasing her. "God, I love you," I breathe into her ear, holding her for as long as I possibly can in this moment.

"Hey," River says, drawing the word out nervously. "So this fuck says the cops are on the way? We may want to leave, like, five minutes ago?"

I grab the keys to the Jeep from my pocket. "Nix?"

He pauses at the passenger door, and I toss the keys to him. "Did hell freeze over?"

I shake my head and walk Rae toward the back door, opening it for her. "Nah. I wanna cuddle with my girl for a while. You fucks have had a lot of time with her, and I miss her."

"I'm glad we could be so considerate of your time, Jackson." Phoenix shakes his head, but I see his lips twitch as he walks around and climbs into the driver's seat.

I snort a laugh and climb in beside Raven, not giving her a chance to put her seatbelt on. Half of her body rests on me when I drag her down on the seat with me. The top of my head rests against the door, and I have to fold my legs, but it doesn't matter.

All that ever matters is this girl in my arms, the guys in the front, and getting free of Maxwell fucking Langston.

RIV

Hey, I'm in the cafeteria now. You want something to eat? There's lots of hot stuff down here. Smells just as good as Nixy's cooking.

Rae. It tells me when you read my texts. Please let me feed you.

I'm not hungry.

RIV

You haven't eaten since yesterday. Don't make me come up there and drag you down here.

A sandwich is fine.

RIV

Better than nothing. How's he doing?

The same.

RIV

And Alexis?

Still screaming down the place, demanding to see him.

RIV

Pierce?

He keeps staring at me like he wants to hold me, but I don't want him to touch me yet. Not now. Not when half of his actions have led to this situation.

RIV

You know it's not his fault that Nix was beat up, Raven.

shrug emoji

RIV

We're all gonna have a talk when I get back
up there. You guys can't hate each other
for the rest of your lives.

CHAPTER FIFTEEN

raven

"We've only got a few more days until we meet with Mark," Phoenix says, voice soft. "I don't know how much we should trust this guy, but if he's the last hope we've got against Maxwell..."

"We won't know until we meet him, Nix," Pierce says, his chest rumbling against my ear. He rubs circles into the skin of my arm, and I nuzzle my face further against his chest. "I'm the one saying we have to have hope."

River laughs. "The world is topsy-turvy if you're the one saying that shit, Pierce."

"Yeah, but after last night..." Pierce blows out a breath, and it fans over my face. "I don't know. I want to be fucking free of all of this and live my life."

"Someone had a road trip epiphany!" River sing-songs.

I can't help but giggle, and Pierce wraps his arms tighter around me.

"Good afternoon, little bird," he says. "We're about twenty minutes out from our hotel."

After stretching my limbs out, I smile at all of my boys. Squeezing between the front seats, I kiss Phoenix's cheek, then River's before sitting back and kissing Pierce's.

Today's gonna be a good fucking day.

"How long have you wanted to go to New Orleans, Rae?" River asks, pulling out my sunglasses and passing them back to me.

I take them with a grateful smile and slide them over my eyes, sighing at the instant relief from the glare of the sun. *Ever since we learned about it in second grade*, I sign.

"She wouldn't shut up about it for a month. I finally added it to our bucket list, and she said she'd make me go with her. As we got older," Pierce grunts when I punch him in the side, rubbing at the spot as he laughs.

"Oh no, now I gotta hear this story," River says and turns in his seat.

I sigh dramatically before signing, *I told him once when I was super high that I dreamed of showing my boobs. Okay? But I was high.*

"You said it sober, too, Blue." Pierce holds his hands up, ready to fight me off again, but I shake my head, biting my lip to hide my smile.

"You aren't gonna show your boobs to anyone but us, Red," Phoenix says.

"Damn straight," River says.

I roll my eyes. I should flash the world just to spite their controlling asses. Would serve them right.

Phoenix pulls into a parking spot in front of our hotel for the night and turns back to us all when he turns off the Jeep. "Everyone, grab a bag and behave. I have no issues getting right back on the highway and ending this stop early."

I push my lower lip out and cross my arms, swatting at him when he tries to push it back.

"Don't be a brat unless you want the punishment," Phoenix says. He gets out and I stare after him, wondering how much trouble I can get myself into tonight.

As we step into our hotel room, I'm grateful for the king bed and not having to pick between my boys. I launch myself on it and splay all of my limbs out, letting out a content sigh.

"Nope," Phoenix says, swatting my ass. "Let's go see the city. We all need exercise."

"Last night wasn't exercise?" River grumbles from the corner of the room.

"No. You traded one car for another, drove for half a minute, then got back into the Jeep." Phoenix turns me over and I grin up at him. "Let's go cross off another bucket list item, Red."

"OH MY FUCKING GOD," River says around a mouthful of pastry. Powdered sugar covers his lips and a little of his cheeks, too.

I laugh and toss my head back in pure pleasure at the taste of cake and sugar they call beignets. I even have a coffee in my hand, because it tastes far more like hot cocoa than I'd have expected.

"Alright," Pierce chuckles as he steps between us. "You're both having public orgasms and we're gonna get arrested for it."

Phoenix comes over and grips my jaw in his hand. Our eyes meet for a second before he leans down and captures my lips with his. He licks the sugar from my mouth before pulling back and winking down at me. "Tastes delicious," he says as he walks a little ahead.

"Oh, look," River says, nearly choking on his food to rush toward a shop. "It's a haunted gift shop."

"I still can't believe this city is that haunted," Phoenix says, glaring at Pierce like it's all his fault.

Pierce holds his hands up. "Rae was the one raving about the ghost stories growing up. We should take one of those haunted tours."

I shake my head and finish my drink before tossing my trash and signing, *I am not up for being scared half to death on this trip.*

"Scared the ghosts will get you, RaeRae?" River chuckles, wrapping his arm around my shoulders and pulling me into him. "I'd protect you."

I pinch his side, making him laugh as we enter the gift shop full of memorabilia for the different spirits known to haunt the streets of New Orleans.

Fake talismans hang everywhere, and there are 'I Survived' stickers for each of the haunted hotels nearby. I hold one up for our hotel, raising a brow at Pierce since he was the one who chose our stop here.

"No ghosts will get us while we're all together," he says. "Promise."

"I wouldn't promise that, if I were you, boy," a woman says from behind the counter.

We all turn toward her, and she smiles, but it's not sweet. Nor is it kind.

It's terrifying. Like she knows more than she'll ever tell another soul.

"Ghosts around here don't care if you're alone or in a group. If you piss one off, they won't stop until they get the revenge they seek." Her voice wavers. She looks to be in her late forties or early fifties. Her hair is a mix of browns and grays, and she's dressed in a plain black dress, the sleeves down to her wrists, skirt falling to her ankles. She looks up at me and her smile falters.

"So what you're saying is that if I want to spend special time with my girl, we might get a ghostly intervention?" River laughs, but everyone else is silent.

The woman keeps staring at me, her oily gaze moving up and down my body until she straightens her spine and moves around the corner.

Pierce places his palm on my lower back, and River moves closer to us, looking down at the woman with a strange expression on his face, as if he knows her.

"You're the missing Langston daughter," she says, lifting her hand to caress my face.

I hold my hand up to stop the boys from intervening, nodding at her as she continues to study me.

"You look so much like them," she whispers. She moves her hand back all of a sudden, as if she realized she shouldn't touch a stranger like this, then clears her throat and steps behind the counter. "You four must come to lunch tomorrow. It's far too late tonight, but tomorrow works fine. I have to close up now, so please take a chocolate as a gift and come back for lunch. Okay?"

I blink a few times, taking a candy as she holds it out, but keeping my gaze on her.

Her hands shake, and she stuffs things inside of a bag

quickly, as if she's got somewhere to be. She wasn't in a hurry when we arrived.

"Why would we have lunch with you?" Pierce asks, his tone harsh and rude.

I glare up at him and narrow my eyes, shaking my head.

"I'm sorry to throw that at you, but I can explain it all tomorrow. Is that okay?" She looks up at me when asking, ignoring the rising anger of my boys, and lets out a breath when I nod.

She ushers us out of the shop, locking the door behind us.

We all turn to watch as the blinds in the windows close, and I tilt my head as I watch her shadow move until it disappears.

"That was fucking weird," Pierce says from beside me. He turns toward us all. "Are we coming for lunch tomorrow, then?"

"She knows something," Phoenix says, looking down at me. "This could be a setup, Red. I don't like it."

"What are the chances Maxwell has someone working in a random gift shop in New Orleans?" Pierce asks, shaking his head as he lets out a small laugh. "Come on, let's go look around some more."

River says nothing as we walk away, and if I've learned anything about him at all, it's that his silence is not to be ignored.

Pierce may be on to something.

Maxwell has friends in all the right places, it seems.

"HOLY FUCK, NO!" River shouts, rushing across the room and picking me up. He carries me back into the bathroom with my hands pounding against his back. "Change into something I'm not tempted to rip off you in public, little vixen. Please. My dick is begging you."

I huff out in annoyance when he places me on the counter, folding my arms and glaring at him. He looks so adorable as he pleads with me, eyes sparkling with horror as if my choice to wear a skintight black dress is going to be his downfall. I make my own damn choices though, so I push him away and slide back down, heading to grab a comfortable set of ankle boots to pair with it.

"Half your ass shows when you bend over, Red," Phoenix says. "I don't like it."

"I like it," Pierce says from the couch.

"You're okay with her going out in public like that?" Phoenix asks him, and I glance behind me to watch them glare at each other.

"Let her show off," Pierce says. "She never had a chance to."

Hello, I sign, *I can do what the fuck I want to do. Shut the fuck up and let's go.* I don't wait for them to reply. I stride right out of the hotel room and stomp down the hall toward the elevator. It may be comfortable to walk on flat land in these boots, but I'm not about to risk my neck by using the stairs.

"Red, we just want to protect—"

I spin around and grip Phoenix's collar, pulling him down to my level so I can glare into his pretty brown eyes before letting him go.

Fuck all of them for thinking they can tell me what to do, or baby me like I can't make my own fucking decisions. Ever.

Or open my own doors.

Or get my own food.

There's a fine line between doting on me and acting as if I can't take care of myself, and they're about to move into the second category.

I tap my foot while I wait for the elevator, feeling their presence at my back as I do. Once we're inside, they all try talking at once, but I hold up my hand to get them to shut the fuck up.

We walk along the streets of New Orleans, and as the minutes go on, I relax again. Taking in the sights and sounds around me, I let myself fall into the culture of The Big Easy. The freedom people have here is something I love. I always told Pierce I wanted to come here during Mardi Gras and get a hundred bead necklaces.

I watch as a woman a few feet away looks up on a balcony and flashes a group of men to get a new set of beads to add to her collection.

"Red, I'm begging you," Phoenix says from beside me.

I flip him off, walk directly to the spot she stood, and pull my dress down enough to show my tits off to the men above me, glaring my own men down.

All three stand speechless as I catch two sets of beads, fix my dress, and put the necklaces on.

Again, I flip the bird as I walk down the street, looking for something to calm my anger.

Hand grenades.

I'd heard about these. An addicting mix of alcohol in a container meant to fuck you up.

Pointing toward the bar where they're being handed out, I wait as Phoenix and Pierce order for our group, then bring four back out.

Before any of them can say anything else, I chug it down, only a little sad when I spill a few drops on my chest.

"Oh, she's big mad," River says with a nervous laugh.

"Yeah," Phoenix says, voice thick with tension. "But so the fuck am I."

Tonight's about to get extremely interesting.

phoenix

She's a dirty little fucking minx right now, and I can't tell if the tension is from all the fucking stress, or from watching her parade around the way she is in the streets of a city known for its debauchery.

I'm half tempted to grab her and have the guys hold her down in a back alley while I fuck her senseless.

The other half of me is head over heels in love with her. I fall deeper each time she stands up to us.

Her defiance is my favorite thing about her.

Today, at least.

"How many necklaces is that?" Pierce asks, slurring his speech a little. I think he's on his third hand grenade, and I should make him stop, but, if he's drunk, it just means he's tapping out for the night.

"Fifteen," I snap, narrowing my eyes at her pretty blues when they stare back at me.

Her dress doesn't have enough stretchy fabric to pull her tits out to begin with, but she's making it work.

"I kinda love her," River says, laughing when she snags a few extra beads in one go.

"She's show-boating," Pierce grumbles. He sips the last of his drink and tosses it into a trash can as we pass it. "I used to get so mad when she did stupid shit in school, but I'm just glad she's getting back to who she was before her mom got sick."

River wraps an arm around Pierce's shoulders. "I never would have thought she was this strong-willed."

"Shouldn't surprise you at all, since you two dickheads assaulted her in the name of revenge and she didn't walk away." I glare at Pierce for a moment and he holds his hands out. "God, you're lucky she forgave you for that shit."

"Will you ever?" he asks, and I scoff.

"I don't know. Not taking part when you're drunk is good enough for me right now." I growl when a guy gets too close to Rae to hand her more beads, and I take long strides toward them both. "Hey baby," I croon, my voice annoying to my own ears.

She looks up at me as she fixes her dress and puts the next set of beads over her neck. *Thank you*, she signs. She's not an idiot, and strange men getting too close is a bad sign for her as much as it is for anyone. She waves the guy off and we walk a little further down the street.

Loud music filters from a club and the low, sensual beat calls to Raven as much as the next set of beads, so we do as we always do.

We follow her.

She pulls me by the arm into the throng of people, and wraps her arms around my neck, pulling me close. Her eyes are glassy from her drinks, but also happiness. True happiness shines there, and I wish we could stay here the rest of the week and forget about Mark Riley and all the shit going on so she could be like this longer.

I wrap my arms around her, grinding my body against hers as I slide my hands down to her ass, pulling her further into me. Leaning down, I kiss her neck and cheek before tugging on her earlobe with my teeth. "I've been thinking about how to punish you all damn night, Red."

She shivers in my hold, and her nails dig into the skin on the back of my neck.

"You want my attention so bad, love?" I growl. I ignore my slip up as we continue to dance. "You've got it."

We dance and drink for another hour, but by the time the crowd becomes more sexual, I pull my crew out and walk us toward our hotel.

I don't make it farther than the elevator before I push Raven up against the wall with my hand around her throat, glaring down at her before slamming my lips to hers. I claim her mouth as much as her body as I shove a hand up her dress and thrust my fingers into her, finding her wet already.

"Damn," River says from behind me, and I open my eyes to see the reflection of Pierce grinding against him, River's fingers in his hair.

Perfect, they'll do their thing while I punish our queen.

The moment the elevator doors open, we hurry our way along the hallway and into our room. She doesn't get a second to breathe or think right now. I'm not the only one livid with her actions, and from the smirk on her face, she orchestrated every second of the night so it would end just like this.

"On your fucking knees, Raven," I order her, pulling back abruptly so she stumbles forward.

She stares up at me as she drops, and the other two stop their shit to watch her do it.

I point. I need no words to let her know what I want her to do. I die a million deaths while she crawls across the floor and toward our bedroom door. She waits patiently, her head hanging with her hair falling over her shoulders as I open it and wait for her to enter.

"Wait at the end of the bed," I command her. The other two lock their eyes on her as they enter the room. I put a finger to my lips and point toward the couch as I lock up.

Stepping up behind Raven, I crouch down behind her and lift her dress, pulling it and all of her fucking necklaces off her and tossing them to the side. I grip the back of her neck and pull her head back until she has to look up at me. A wicked grin stretches my lips when she swallows anxiously. "Nervous, Red?"

She nods, shifting on her knees, squirming beneath me.

"You fucking should be." I shove her head forward and reach for some necklaces, twisting them between my fingers. "Boys?"

River and Pierce walk to my side, and I hand them some beads before sending them back to the couch.

"She has to earn a necklace from each of us tonight. After that, we'll forgive her for searching for gifts from other men." I whip one necklace at her back, and she jolts at the small sting. "Color?" I ask.

She taps the bed in front of her once, then signs, *Green.*

"Good girl," I praise. "I'm going to sit on this chair and wait for you to earn the beads from the other two, then you'll crawl to me and do as I ask. Understand?"

She looks up to meet my eyes and nods, a small smile threatening her lips before I swing the necklace at her ass.

"Don't get sassy now, Red. You've made us chase after you all damn night, seeing you flaunt that body to others. You may own us outside of the bedroom, beautiful, but we own you inside of it. Now," I sit back and fold my hands together, nodding toward River without another word.

Raven takes a deep breath to center herself, then turns toward River and crawls to him.

He groans and shifts on the couch, his hands clenching on the cushions. "You're so beautiful, RaeRae."

She sits in between his knees, and Pierce reaches out to run his hand through her hair. He looks down at her with such love in his eyes. I'd be jealous if I didn't know exactly how he was feeling.

"Hands off, pup," River tells him. "You're drunk, so you don't get to touch her."

Pierce sighs and sits back, folding his arms.

"You wanna earn some beads, little vixen?" River asks, shifting his gaze between Raven and Pierce.

She nods.

"Work with him to get me off," is his only command.

I wait and watch, intrigued, as Raven and Pierce work to remove River's pants, pulling out his hard dick before descending on it as if they've been hungry for it for hours.

My dick throbs when Raven's ass sways in the air as she works to get River off. Her hands move between her thighs, and I snap, "Hands off, Red. This isn't about you right now."

She spins her head around to glare at me, and I chuckle darkly. Her eyes widen just before she turns back around to work River over.

River's groans become louder while Pierce and Raven share his dick between them, and he caresses both of their heads with love shining in his eyes.

"Fuck yes," he groans, tossing his head back. "Take all of it. Fuck, fuck, fuck," he chants over and over until his hips surge from the couch as he finishes.

Pierce pulls up first, earning a kiss from River before River leans down and kisses Raven. He takes both his and Pierce's necklaces and places them over her neck before spinning her and sending her my way.

Her lips are swollen, her eyes are glassy, and if I checked, she'd be soaked.

I caress her head for a few seconds, guiding her toward my thigh where she lays her cheek. As I take in my options for a moment, I let her rest.

"You were such a good girl for them, Red. Are you ready to be a good girl for me?" I run my thumb along her cheek before pushing it into her mouth, inhaling sharply when she sucks on it and nods in response to my question. "Get on the bed," I whisper.

I grab a few more necklaces and bring them along with me, stripping myself along the way. "Take off your under-wear," I tell her, and she does so quickly before resuming her position on all fours on the bed. "Color?" I ask, and she reaches her hands out to sign *Green*. "Good girl," I praise her once more.

I whip her with a necklace and mark one of her ass cheeks with it, then the other, in rapid succession until there's a patterned design of beads along her ass. She's squirming so much the sheets bunch beneath her and her breathing is labored as she tries to maintain her position.

"Did you enjoy flaunting yourself all over the streets tonight, Red?" There's a bite to my tone, an anger. I don't want her to act like that, but what I want doesn't matter in the grand scheme of things. I'm allowed to be jealous, but I don't control her. Not outside the bedroom.

She looks back at me and nods, trying to hold back the smile she wants to let loose.

"I know you enjoyed torturing us with it. You had too much fun when you showed your tits to everyone who wanted to see." I swat her ass with the beads again, grinning when she flinches. "I think you wanted the punishment more than you wanted their attention." I swat her again. "Is that true, Red? Did you *want* me to turn this little ass black and blue tonight?"

She nods, her eyes boring into mine.

"Did you want my attention?" I ask, wincing when I think of the times I've spent on this trip lost in my own thoughts.

She takes a deep breath and nods again.

I swat her a few more times in silence before climbing onto the bed behind her and pulling the last necklace over her head. "You've got my attention, Raven. What do you want to do with it?" I nip at her ear as I splay my body against hers, keeping my weight off of her.

She looks back at me, and I wipe the tear that falls from her lashes before turning her onto her back. I peer down into her eyes as I thrust inside of her, pulling one of her legs up over my forearm. "Did you want me to fuck you ruthlessly?" I thrust a little harder into her until her head lightly smacks the headboard.

She shakes her head, biting her lip as she curls her arm around my neck. Tugging me down, she presses her lips firmly to mine.

I kiss her back as I slow my hips, sliding in and out of her.

I make love to her for the first time, allowing our souls to merge.

After I pull back from our kiss, I wrap both of her legs around my waist, then rest my forearms next to her head and tangle my hands in her hair. I look into her eyes, finding hers locked onto mine. My heart melts for hers as I ply her body into a slow rolling orgasm, holding her beneath me.

She arches her back, and as she opens her mouth on a silent scream, I kiss her like I'll never get another chance to.

As she finishes, I thrust into her a few more times before finding my release and holding her in my arms until they shake with the effort of holding me up.

When I glance down at her, her tears conflict with her smile, and I wipe them away.

I don't say a word as I pull out of her and pull her into my arms, then slide off the bed and head for the bathroom.

River and Pierce are sound asleep curled up on the couch, and I keep our girl to myself for a while longer.

I have an idea for tomorrow and I want you to hear me out.

Sorry. Please, will you hear me out?

RAERAE

I suppose I can. What's your idea?

Don't kill me.

RAERAE

raised eyebrow emoji What's your idea, River Jacobs?

So... it's been a while since you and Pierce have done much of anything. You've hugged him like... twice... in two months.

RAERAE

?????

If we gave you all the control tomorrow night. All of it. Down to every last movement anyone makes... will you let him join in?

Rae?

Baby...?

Shit. I didn't mean to make you mad. It was just an idea.

RAERAE

I can have ALL of the control?

Yes! Every last movement is up to you.

RAERAE

And if I want to do nothing at all? Or if I want to stop midway through?

151

It's all your decision.

RAERAE

Promise me he won't have any control at all
and I'll let him in.

raven

Analyzing what just happened between Phoenix and me is going to make my head spin more than it already does on a regular basis, but I can't help but feel a little overwhelmed with the change.

He changed from this dominating sexual god to someone I'd completely fallen in love with.

In seconds.

I mean, it's been more than seconds that I've been in love with him, sure, but watching that shift in his eyes, his body movements, the way he held me?

It drove me to the brink of tears.

I shiver when he sets me down on the counter, and he apologizes for the cold with a soft kiss before turning toward the big jacuzzi tub.

He turns it on, and the sound of the water fills the silence.

Not awkward silence. Not painful silence.

Blissful, yet hesitant silence.

We've stolen a moment of peace amid all of our chaos, and neither one of us is sure how long it will last.

The smell of strawberry soda wafts through the room, and I smile when Phoenix grabs me and pulls me into the water with him, my back against one end of the tub and his against the other. He pulls my feet into his lap and massages them and my calves, grinning shyly at me.

We just stare at each other for a few moments before he asks me to stand and turn around so he can inspect the impact marks from our play.

"These will be gone in the morning," he says. He runs his soapy hands over my cheeks, down and back again before turning me. He looks up at me and chews his lip for a moment. "How are you feeling?" he asks.

Great, I sign. *It didn't hurt more than I wanted it to, and crawling to you was hot.*

He chuckles and shakes his head. "You're something else, Raven Hill."

The way he looks at me and says my name is intoxicating.

He draws me down to sit in the water again and drags me between his thighs as our eyes meet. "I need to tell you something, Raven."

He never says my name.

Nervous Phoenix is new. Adorable.

Our eyes meet, and he takes a deep breath. "I love you, Raven. More than I ever thought possible. You're everything to me. I know you come as a package deal with Pierce and River, and I don't care. I'm here for the long haul with you, beautiful." He looks down and lifts my hands between us to kiss my knuckles before looking up at me.

My heart pounds a million miles a second as I stare at

him, then I mouth 'I love you too' before plastering myself to his chest and kissing him, our lips and teeth clashing as we slide through the tub, the sound of his light laughter echoing around us.

"ARE we sure we need to go see this chick?" River asks, again, as we walk up the street toward the haunted gift shop.

I tuck my shirt into my jeans and shake my arms out. I'm too fucking nervous to have lunch with a stranger, but she knew of me and if she knows anything useful, we need to get it out of her.

Phoenix suggests as much to River, who sighs and continues walking behind us.

"Should we record this conversation?" Pierce asks, and everyone turns to look at him. "What?"

"You asked permission before doing something that would affect the whole group," River says. "It's a miracle. You're growing up!"

"Shut up," Pierce grumbles as he pushes River away.

It might be a good idea, I sign just as we step in front of the shop.

Before I open the door, I take a deep breath, then walk inside to the sound of the bells clinking overhead.

"I'll be with you in just a moment," the woman calls from behind the counter.

We step further into the room, and as she stands to her full height, she perks up, closing a drawer loudly before rounding the corner. She pulls me into her arms, hugging me as if we've known each other our whole lives.

"Be good boys and lock the door, will you? We'll go back and have lunch." She wraps her thin arms around me and drags me further into the shop until we have to ascend a staircase. "Go on now, dear."

I take a few steps, exhaling when I hear one boy's boots hitting the stairs, too. At the top, I walk into what looks to be a cramped apartment. A kitchen and living area are open floor plan, with two closed doors I assume are the bathroom and bedroom.

"My name is Adeline Winfield. I apologize for not telling you sooner." She walks inside of the small kitchen and grabs mugs from a cupboard. "You all have a seat, and I'll get you something to drink."

She doesn't ask what we want, and that unsettles me, but I take a seat next to Phoenix on the couch, clutching his hand as we wait.

River and Pierce come upstairs a few seconds later and sit down on Phoenix's other side. I watch as they both cast their eyes over her apartment.

Fairly empty.

Nothing of value.

Nothing personal.

Something is up here, and we need to be careful.

"Should we just get out of here?" Pierce questions.

"All information is good information right now," Phoenix whispers back, casting a charming smile up at Adeline as she enters the living room with a tray of drinks and cookies.

"I hope some warm tea is fine with you all. I quit drinking coffee years ago. It was aging me faster than I wanted." She sets the drinks down on the table as the boys mumble their thanks. She purses her lips as she glances up at me and her brow furrows. "You don't talk much, do you, dear?"

"She's mute, ma'am," Phoenix tells her. "Lost her voice a little over a year ago."

"What a shame," Adeline states with a shake of her head. She grabs her own drink and sits on a recliner next to the couch, casting a glance around our group. "You're all so charming. It's very sweet. Reminds me of the boys I used to see when I attended c-college." She sips her tea from her glass, and I narrow my eyes when her hands tremble.

Why is she scared?

I lean against Phoenix and pretend to take a drink.

"Smart girl," he whispers into my ear before kissing my temple.

"Miss Adeline," Pierce says, placing his mug down on the table before sitting up straight and looking at her with kind eyes.

"Ah!" She looks into her own cup before looking at us all again, a forced smile on her face. "I'm sorry for being so secretive. I simply wanted to meet the missing Langston daughter. Has he found you yet? Your father?"

I nod, hesitant to let her know too much information.

"I'll bet he's ecstatic. Maxwell was such a charming young man. It ruined him when that witch Everlyn took you, dear. He was absolutely devastated. I suppose you were under the one stone he hadn't turned over." She sighs and shakes her head before sipping from her drink. "Dears, you should drink your tea!"

"You know, Miss Adeline, I don't think we will. We've hydrated enough this morning." Pierce stands and helps

River up before looking down at her. "Are you going to be a problem for us?"

"Pierce," Phoenix admonishes quietly, smiling at the woman. "I apologize. We've had a long few days on our spring break trip."

"I don't suppose I would be a problem if you'd drink your tea. It's rude to come into my home and not drink what I offer you." Adeline narrows her beady little eyes at Pierce. "He said you would be trouble for me."

"We need to go," Phoenix grits out, standing and pulling me with him.

"But he's coming for you. You know that, right?" Adeline calls, her voice stronger than it was before.

"Get your ass downstairs, Raven," Pierce tells me.

I look at him and River, then point to them both before gesturing to the stairs, hoping they'll come with us.

"Go," Pierce shouts, and I jump.

Phoenix grabs my arms and pulls me with him toward the stairs. I struggle, wanting to stay inside with them so I know they're safe.

River's eyes glaze over, and I worry about him the entire way down the stairs and out of the shop.

river

"River," Pierce says, shaking my shoulder, but I shake my head as sit back down and glare at Adeline.

"I recognize you, boy," she says, a twisted smile lighting up her face.

My gut rolls.

"You're Robert Jacobs' son, aren't you?" She places her mug down on the table and leans forward.

Pierce grabs my arm, but I push him away. I study her dark eyes. The same dark eyes that tried to tell me how sick I was for wanting another boy when I was in middle school. The same dark eyes who looked at me with pity while my father assaulted me in his office at the church...

"CLOSE THE DOOR, RIVER," *my father commands as I enter his office. He doesn't glance up from the Bible in his*

hands, and I wonder if this is the day I burn the fucking thing to ashes.

"Yes, sir," I say. The door closes with a snick and I rest my forehead against it before turning around and forcing my lips into a smile. There's nothing more I can do to save myself right now.

Not yet, anyway.

"Only five new children gave themselves to God this month, son." He looks up at me from over his glasses, and I shift uncomfortably on my feet. "Sit," he commands. I plop down in the chair in front of his desk.

"I'm trying my hardest, father, but—"

"I'm growing more and more frustrated with you, River. You aren't doing what I'm asking of you, and it's a shame I have to keep punishing you." He places his Bible down, and I stare at the leather cover and worn edges as he makes his way around the desk, unbuckling his belt as he goes. "Punishments teach you lessons. Isn't that right?"

I nod my head, and he smacks the side of my face. "Y-yes, sir," I say, meeting his eyes as I do.

"Pull down your pants, son. I hate to do this, but I have to punish you. It's my role as a father, yes?" He snaps his belt together when I take too long to answer.

Keeping my eyes on his, I nod. "Yes, sir."

"If you cry, I'll make this harder, River, so keep that shit to yourself."

Tonight's the first night I've practiced dissociating, and so far, it's working. I wince and groan, but I let my mind go to a different place. A place where I don't have to feel any of this, not really.

When he's finished, he pats me on the head like I'm a good boy, and my blood boils with rage. I grab the pocket knife I've been carrying around and clutch it in my hand, but ultimately decide not to use it, letting it fall back against my thigh as I turn and walk away.

"Have Miss Winfield clean those marks so they don't stick around," he orders me as I open the door.

I turn to face him, meeting his too satisfied gaze as I say, once again, "Yes, sir." I exit the room, wincing at the all-consuming pain in the lower half of my body, and enter Miss Winfield's office.

She points to the cabinets where the first aid materials are, without looking at me.

I grab the box with my name on it, because of course that's how sick this place is, and place it on her desk, standing as still as I can manage while I wait for her to move.

She sighs like I'm the biggest annoyance to her, then places her book down and looks up at me with judgment simmering in her gaze. "Why do you insist on making him mad?"

My laugh echoes around us as I turn around, undoing my pants as I go. "I can't make people do what they don't want to do, Miss Winfield."

"River," she sighs and begins applying ointments. I hear her intake of breath at the added blood tonight. "You should get your body used to this treatment. I'll send you home with reading materials. How to prepare yourself. I would hate for him to accidentally kill you."

"As opposed to killing me on purpose?" I toss my hands in the air. "God forbid it's an accident."

She swats my sore ass, and I whip around to glare at her. She glares right back. "Do not use God's name in vain, boy. Now turn around so I can fix you up. You can go pray for forgiveness when I'm done with you."

I do as I'm told, again, and wonder if I should be praying for forgiveness... or vengeance.

"I HATE YOU," I spit, standing and knocking my mug out of my lap. The warm liquid splashes out as the glass shatters on the ground.

"Hate is such a strong word, River. Surely your father taught you that." She shakes her head and chuckles as she leans back in her chair.

"What do you want?" I ask, clenching and unclenching my fists at my sides. I'd like to kill her, but no one asked me, so I keep that thought in my head.

She never helped, she only let him keep going, sending others away as they entered the church. She held the fort down while my dad held me down.

"I want nothing but the missing Langston heir, that's all. Maxwell is looking for her."

"Maxwell found her last year," Pierce snaps, grabbing my wrist and making me sit down.

"Oh no, he's searching for her now. Offering a prize to anyone who can find her." Adeline pulls out a piece of paper and passes it to Pierce.

He takes it and sits back down.

On it is a picture of Raven underneath the word MISS-ING. It implicates us as her kidnappers, half-assed mugshots and all.

Pierce barks out a loud laugh and stuffs the paper in his jeans. "Maxwell cannot be fucking serious about this."

"Oh, he's terribly serious. Always has been. All I had to

do was tell him you were here and when. He should be here in the next half hour or so." She shrugs as if none of this shit bothers her.

"He's going to *sell her*!" I yell, jumping over the table to get to her.

Mugs and plates go flying, and Pierce grabs me around the waist, pulling me back. The wood cracks and collapses as I fight him, and he stands up, dragging me toward the stairs.

"I won't fucking forget your name, Adeline Winfield," Pierce warns her. "You just made my shit list."

"Better yours than Maxwell's, boy." She calls, and I don't miss the sound of her laughter as we descend the stairs.

We pause in the middle of the shop and Pierce grabs hold of my face, looking me in the eye.

I shift uncomfortably, trying to avoid his stare, but he holds me in a painful grip.

"Look at me," he snaps, so I relent, letting the frustrated tears fall. "We won't let them take her. I swear it. Let's get the fuck out of here and pick up our shit from the hotel. We have to leave."

I nod and bounce on the balls of my feet, wanting to run as far from here as possible but also rush back in there and—

"River!" Pierce yells in my face, and I flinch. "Get it together. Come on. Let's go."

I nod a few times. "Yeah. Yeah, let's go."

He ushers me out of the shop, and we walk up to Phoenix and Raven.

She steps out of Phoenix's embrace and wraps herself around me, clutching the back of my shirt until I bundle her in my arms. She buries her face in my chest and I let out a deep breath of relief.

"Come on," Pierce says, wrapping an arm over my shoulders.

He fills them both in on the rest of our visit with Adeline, and when we make it to the hotel, we pack up as fast as possible and toss our things into a rental car we requested Lance get to us as soon as he could.

"I'll keep the Jeep safe," Lance says as Pierce hands him the keys. "Get lost for a while. Don't head straight for Riley."

Pierce nods and watches as Phoenix slides into the backseat with Raven. "We planned to hit up Universal Studios."

"A theme park could be good," Lance says. "I'll put a few more guys on you, so you'll feel watched, but don't worry about it. I'm gonna backtrack and lose Langston."

Nodding, Pierce looks at me and pulls me into a hug. "I'm so sorry you put up with so much stupid shit, man. Fuck."

I pat Pierce on the back and turn back toward the car. After I nod to Lance, I climb inside and rest my head against the seat. I could forget everything if the world swallowed me up. I jump when a hand squeezes my shoulder, relaxing when I turn to see Raven looking at me with worried eyes.

"Don't worry about it, Raven. She was a witch. We need a good plan to get back at these fucks." I squeeze her fingers tightly in mine and relax as I close my eyes.

I plan to sleep until we make it to the theme park, then hope I die falling off a roller coaster.

It'd be an epic way to die.

RIV

Did you enjoy what you saw, Raven?

Don't play shy now, baby girl. We both
saw you.

Did Nixy boy help you out up there? I'm
sure you got wet watching him suck me off.

Rae... I can hear you. You may not be able
to talk, baby, but I can hear it when your
breathing picks up. My texts making it hard
for you to think?

Are you wet for me?

Answer me. Tell me what you're thinking...
or doing.

Seeing you both like that turned me on so
much. Nix left to take a phone call... and
I've been left a little *needy*.

RIV

Fuck. Let me come up there and get
you off?

What would you do to me, Mr. Jacobs?

RIV

Damnit, Rae. I'd come up there and fuck
you senseless, that's what. I'd try to take
my time with you, but then, because there's
nothing in the world that could stop me
from pleasing you, I'd do things to your
body you've only dreamt of.

I dream a lot, Riv.

RIV

Let me bring them to life for you, Raven.

Come up here, then, before my vibrator does the job you want to do.

raven

"Oh my god, my legs are so fucking stiff," River complains as he drags himself out of the rental, stretching his limbs dramatically as he walks toward the front of the hotel. "Did we have to drive for nine straight hours?"

Pierce rolls his eyes and stretches before helping me from the back seat. He kisses my forehead before releasing me so he can help Phoenix unload our bags from the trunk. "Safest and fastest way to get here was to not stop."

I walk up to River and wrap my arm around his waist, smiling when he relaxes even a little in my hold.

The drive from New Orleans to Orlando was a long, quiet, and tense one. Pierce was lead-footed for most of it, and I'm surprised no one pulled us over. But we're here, and this is the last fun stop of our vacation, and I'm determined to pretend like nothing with Adeline Winfield ever happened.

At least for tonight and tomorrow.

Phoenix and Pierce lead the way into the hotel, grab our keys, and walk us down the hall to our room for the night.

River stops short when he sees the glass wall showing a pool inside.

A pool with a sign that clearly says it's closed for the evening.

"River," Pierce barks, glaring back at him. "No."

"Come on!" River groans. "You guys steal all the fun."

I press my face against his side and giggle as we follow the other two toward our room. He's not wrong, but we don't need the extra attention right now of getting caught in a closed hotel pool.

River grabs his suitcase and plops it down on one of the queen beds, rifling through it until he pulls out his swim trunks. He strips without another word and puts them on before heading toward the door. When he glances back at me, he winks, then smacks the top of the doorframe and walks down the hall.

"He's gonna get himself arrested," Phoenix says in a monotone, staring at Pierce.

"You act like he's my responsibility." Pierce folds his arms over his chest, then looks over at me. "Why are you laughing? We're not going."

I stand and walk to my own bag, then dig through it until I find my bikini. The guys continue to protest while I change into it, but just as I turn down the hallway, Pierce growls and his footsteps echo around us as he rushes after me. I take off like a bolt of lightning down the carpeted corridor, laughing the entire way. When I look back and see Phoenix racing after me too, my laughter grows and grows until I'm in fits of it.

Our circumstances may have forced us to grow up too

fast, but we still know how to have fun when the time is right.

River's already splashing around in the water when we enter the room, and Pierce lifts me over his shoulder as he passes me, then tosses me in the deep end, laughing the entire time.

It feels so good to hear him laugh.

I surface and reach my arms out, splashing him where he stands on the edge. *Get in so I can have proper revenge*, I sign, glaring at him with faux anger.

"Oh I will, after I wait and see if your top's actually gonna fall off."

I gasp and glance down at my chest, only to find it firmly in place. When I peer back up at him, Phoenix is at his side and they're both laughing. River joins in and pulls me into his arms, pulling me away and toward the other side of the pool.

"It's okay, little vixen. I'll keep you safe from the big bad monsters." He buries his face in my neck, growling, and I wrap my arms around his at my stomach, closing my eyes and breathing him in.

"Did he just call us monsters, Nix?" Pierce shouts.

"I think he did." Phoenix grins and his eyes rake over me as I squirm in River's hold.

They're gonna fuck me up tonight. I can sense it.

"Guess we better act like monsters," Pierce says before he jumps into the water.

I let out a silent scream and slide out of River's arms, swimming to the opposite side of the pool as fast as I can. Right as I reach the ladder, Phoenix's arms band around my waist and he pulls me back.

He lifts me up and tosses me over to Pierce, who has his arms wide open, waiting for me.

River swims toward him, tackling him down into the water by the head. His laughter echoes while Pierce spits water out each time he surfaces.

We're a mess, me and this crew. But damn if we aren't a beautiful one.

I laugh breathlessly as the boys tackle each other, trying to keep from being dunked. The tension leaves us in this small space of time, and in its place is the sense of love, friendship, and youth.

It's the only way I want life to be when we get all of this sorted out.

"What the hell are you doing?"

We all freeze and snap our heads toward the loud male voice coming from the doorway.

He sighs and rubs the bridge of his nose before scratching his pudgy belly. Shaking his head, he points toward the door. "Just... leave. It's been a long night already. Get the hell out of the pool."

"Yes, sir," River says, saluting the guy. He swims over to the edge and I watch as all three of my guys' muscles flex as they climb out. "Can't believe you talked us into this, Rae! Got us in trouble and everything." He clicks his tongue and shakes his head at me as he helps me stand, laughing when I swat at his chest.

Phoenix wraps a towel around my shoulders and Pierce grabs my hand as we walk back toward our room.

We all dry off and change into comfortable clothes, the boys push the beds together, and we lay down nestled as close as physically possible with smiles on our faces.

Despite the mounting issues we're facing, I wish every single day could be like this.

THE SMELL of waffles and coffee permeate the air, and I roll over and glare at the sunlight streaming through the window. Damn sun's not even risen yet, and it's already hot on my skin. I sigh and roll onto my back, staring up at the ceiling. River's smiling face pops up into my field of vision, and I can't help but smile.

"Good morning, little vixen. Are you ready for a fun day filled with death-defying rides and sugar to your heart's content?" He waggles his brows like the goof he is.

I sit up and reach my hands out for the orange juice he poured me, relaxing against the headboard in the middle of the two beds.

"We've got thirty minutes," Phoenix says as he walks in from the shower.

I sip from my glass as I bask in all the glorious tattooed skin he has on display, licking my lip when a bit of juice–or maybe that was drool–falls past my lip.

It doesn't take long to finish breakfast and get changed, especially with the excitement of a theme park ahead of us. We're able to get lost in a sea of people for a while.

"Lance has about five guys on our asses today," Pierce says from the front seat. He grabs my hand in his and kisses my knuckles, smiling over at me. "We're safe today. We can cross off another bucket list item."

"Is this one as naughty as the last one?" River asks, placing his head between the seats and looking at us both.

"Nope," Pierce says. "This one is just to come here. We've both always wanted to, but we live so far away, and it was never in the cards financially."

As we pull up to the park, I study the plethora of roller coasters in the distance. Paired with all the people already here at nine in the morning, I'm amazed by the beauty of this place, even if it's crowded to all hell.

Phoenix insisted we all wear matching tops so we could find each other quicker, just in case. We all dressed in black shirts with a raven on the back, its wings spread mid-flight. Nothing else identifies us, so we're safe to just exist today.

Good thing, too, since we meet Mark Riley in the morning.

I take a deep breath and hold tight to Pierce's hand when he grabs mine, tugging me past the entrance lane after showing off our tickets on his phone.

"Where to first, Blue?" he asks, pausing in the middle of the chaos to wait for my answer.

I take in all the different themed rides from my favorite movies, then find the biggest rollercoaster I can, and point it out to the guys. Pierce swallows nervously, and I smile when he nods and takes a step in that direction.

Thank god for our fast passes, because the line is already long, and they've only been open for ten minutes.

"I'm saying no alcohol today," Phoenix says as he leans against the railing. When we all glance over at him, he shrugs. "It's a dumb idea with all the rides you guys want to go on. Not to mention I don't want to deal with anyone's hangovers when we meet Riley tomorrow."

"Alright," River chimes in, wrapping his arm around Phoenix's shoulders. "We're gonna not talk about that right now. We'll get on this ride, and if we *don't* die on it, we're gonna enjoy the day. No talks about Riley, Langston, Rapture. None of it. We're safe, right, Pierce?"

Pierce pulls his phone from his pocket, tapping away for a few seconds before putting it back and nodding at River.

"See, Nixy-boy? Safe." River pats his shoulder and moves forward in line. "Let's enjoy our queen and ignore all the other shit today."

"You're up," calls one worker.

I turn and take a deep breath before climbing into the seat and buckling myself in while River claims the spot right next to me.

"You ready for this, RaeRae? We could die on this ride."

I glare at him, and he laughs in response. My hair falls in front of my face as I shake my head and wiggle my body around, letting go of all the fear just before the ride moves.

"Hey, if we don't make it," River says, "there's something I want to tell you."

I kick his shin and clench my fists around the bars in front of my chest as we move at an angle so sharp my stomach revolts. The sky is bright and the clouds are gorgeous from up here. I draw in a deep breath when the coaster stills at the top, then let it out gradually.

We'll survive this ride, but will we make it to the end of this year?

As we careen down the first drop from the roller coaster, I let out a silent scream, all the air leaving my lungs, and all the thoughts scrambling in my brain.

If we do make it to the end of this year, I want to feel as free as this every single day.

river

Everyone's laughing, having a great time. It's great.

Totally great.

Really great, actually.

"Okay, so the show was really good." Pierce looks down at Rae and I watch her face shift into this expression of pure love for him.

I'm only a little jealous, but then she turns the same on me and I break out into a giant grin. I'm one thousand percent sure I love this girl. As we walk toward a row of food stands, I toss my arm over her shoulders and pull her into my side. "I liked the show, too. Some of the special effects were a bit too realistic." I laugh and shake my head. "Could make anything fake look real."

Rae shifts her hands in front of her and signs, *That's the point of it all. To get you to believe in something you normally wouldn't.*

I kiss her temple. *I believe in my love for you*, I think. To myself, of course. Telling her I love her seems like a more terrifying prospect than confronting my father or trying to fix my trauma.

"Why don't we just order a pizza?" Pierce asks, already standing in line for it.

"Yeah, no," Phoenix replies, stuffing his phone back into his pocket. He looks between us, then points to a deli. "We don't need this much grease in our stomachs while we ride the coasters." He takes off toward the place, no doubt expecting us to follow.

Rae hesitates for a moment, then moves ahead to catch up with him, turning her megawatt smile on him when he pulls her into his side.

"He wants us to eat sandwiches?" I sigh.

Pierce wraps his arm around my shoulders, much like I did Rae, and walks with me toward the others. "No one wants to yak on a coaster, Riv."

When we reach the front of the line, I reluctantly order a sandwich with my crew.

"I don't want to ride it," Phoenix says as he tosses his food wrapper away twenty minutes later. "I really, really don't." He looks at Rae as if she'll let him free of the largest coaster in the park.

"Are you giving our girl puppy dog eyes over there, Nixy boy?" I laugh loudly and slap the table as I stare at him. "This is the best day ever."

Rae glares at me before lifting her hands and signing, *Stop picking on him.*

"Never, sweet girl. I'll remember this forever." I lean back and fold my arms over my chest as I watch their exchange.

They decide that we'll go on a few more rides before we head off to that one, if only to let our stomachs settle.

See? Fucking responsible.

Gross.

Pierce and Rae walk ahead of us. They're busy having some argument in sign language I can't see, so I walk beside Phoenix, sighing when I see him on his phone again. Reaching over, I try to snatch it from his hands, and he shoves me in the shoulder.

"Hands off, Jacobs," Phoenix growls before stuffing his phone into his pocket.

"What in the hell is more important than spending vacation time doing vacation things?" I ask, folding my arms over my chest as I stare him down.

"The trial for Lexi's murder is happening next week."

"So? That's *next* week, not this week. And it's not today, either."

He shoves both of his hands into his pockets and stares straight ahead, his brows furrowed in frustration.

"Is there something else going on, Nixy boy?" I ask. "Why the hell are you so torn up over this shit?"

He shrugs, then blows out a heavy breath. "My old crew—the band—they're all a little fucked up about it, too. She was a part of us, even if we hated her at the end. It just stings a lot more than I thought."

"If she went to prison for the rest of her life, what would you think? Isn't death better than that?" I don't understand why he's fucked up about this, because the bitch killed his family and they let her off after six months in a psych ward. She deserved worse, and she finally got it. Murdered or not.

"She would have gotten better if she were in prison." He looks up at the sky as we continue to walk behind Rae and Pierce. "I don't wish the worst for people. Not really. Hell, the guy she was with is being accused of her murder, and I don't wish that shit on him, either."

"Wait, wait, wait," I say, putting my hand on his shoulder to stop him. "The guy that put you in the hospital? Xavier Hayes? What the *fuck,* man! He could have killed you! You absolutely should wish that shit on him!"

"I don't expect anyone to understand. That's why I've been talking to my old crew. I'm leaving you guys out of it so you don't have to stress out." He pulls away from me and starts walking to catch up to the other two, and I shake my head as I follow.

I'll never understand the human need to make everyone happy, even if those people have fucked us over before.

If I ever get my hands on that guy again, I'd beat him harder than he did Phoenix on New Year's Eve. I'm already mad Phoenix didn't do the same when he visited him in jail before we left.

Missed opportunities and all that.

"RAE," I laugh, holding her still as she continues to wobble on her own feet. "Give it a few seconds, sweet girl."

"That was the third spinning ride we've been on in a row," Phoenix says. "If we don't take a break, one of us will puke."

"Ice cream?" Pierce asks, pointing toward a stand.

We all agree and get in line to order. Rae sits down next to me at an empty picnic table in the grassy area. She looks as beautiful as ever with her hair fucked to all hell from the wind.

I grin and tilt my ice cream, gasping dramatically as a few drops of the sugary goodness fall onto her exposed shoulder. "Oh shit! I'm *so* sorry," I tell her. She stares up at me with a raised brow and I laugh.

"The fuck, Riv?" Pierce asks, only to chuckle when I do it again.

I shrug and meet his gaze. "I guess I gotta clean her up now. My bad, RaeRae." I reach for a napkin, but at the last second I toss it on the table, grab her jaw in my fingers and tilt her head to the side. With the patience of a saint, I lean down and let my breath fan across her heated skin until goosebumps pebble along her throat. The sugar has nothing against the taste of her on my tongue as I drag it along her shoulder, toward her neck, and back again.

She shivers in my hold and I listen as her breathing hitches, grinning when she struggles to hold her own ice cream.

"River," Pierce barks.

I look up at him and wink before sitting up straight and taking another bite of ice cream as if nothing ever happened.

Rae lets out a shaky breath and licks her ice cream, keeping her eyes cast toward the table as she struggles to hold back her smile. Her cheeks are almost as red as her hair.

"We're in public," Phoenix says with a sharp tone, but his lips twitch as he takes in Rae's flustered state.

"I don't care if we're standing in front of the Pope. I'd lick our girl anywhere and everywhere."

Rae smacks my shoulder, and I laugh as I glance down to meet her gaze. She shakes her head and bites into her ice cream with a tad more aggression than she needs to.

"The hell?" Pierce asks a few minutes later when we're walking toward the final coaster ride of our night. The big one. Phoenix doesn't want to go on it, but we're getting him on it one way or another.

"What's up?" I ask, stepping up to his side.

He shows me his caller ID, and I raise a brow when I see Agent Starling's name on it.

"Better answer it," I tell him, stuffing my hands into my pockets. I don't know if Starling calling right now is a good or a bad thing, since only Pierce has handled this guy since before Valentine's Day.

Pierce pulls me over to sit on a bench off to the side and puts the call on speakerphone. Rae and Phoenix follow, and I pull Rae into my lap as I wait to hear what this call is about.

"Afternoon, Agent Starling," Pierce answers. I raise a brow at the formality.

"Jackson," Starling greets him. "We've got a lot of information we're wading through. Tons of evidence. I need," he stops speaking, then sighs and clears his throat.

"Absolutely not," Pierce interrupts him, shaking his head and glaring at the device in his hand. "I said no before and I'll keep saying no, Starling."

The man lets out a long sigh. "I need as much help from your crew as possible. You guys are the ones with the most information."

"We can leave Raven out of it," Pierce says.

"We can't, son."

"I'm not your fucking son. And we can leave her out of it. I told you we will, so we will." Pierce starts to hang up, but Agent Starling calls out for him to wait.

"Listen," he says. "We could take them all down, but you guys are going to have to help me out with this and come in to see me. Or I can meet you at your place. Or a different place." He blows out a breath and I imagine him shaking his head and running his fingers over his mustache. "I need statements, and I'll need you for testimonies."

Rae looks over at Pierce. *I want to take them down, Pierce. Tell him I'll be there.*

Pierce watches Rae for a while before nodding his head and leaning forward to kiss her once. He pulls back and looks down at the phone like it might explode.

"Next week," he answers. "We'll meet you just outside our place."

"I was kind of hoping I could meet you guys in the next few days," Starling says hesitantly, as if he's scared Pierce might rescind his agreement.

"We're out of town right now," Pierce tells him.

"Ah, it is spring break, isn't it?" Starling chuckles. "Well, call me when you're back in town and we'll set something up. And kids?" he calls right as Pierce attempts to hang up on him.

"What's up, Starling?" Pierce asks, exasperated.

"Be careful. Watch your backs, got it?"

"Got it," Pierce says. He hangs up and stuffs his phone in his pocket.

"Well," I say with a nervous laugh. "That was ominous as fuck."

"You do realize us going in means you have to talk about your dad, right River?" Pierce looks into my eyes, and I can't tell if he's trying to rile me up or if he's making sure I know what's going to happen.

I shrug one shoulder and lift Rae off my lap before grabbing her hand and starting toward the line for the coaster. "I'll be fine."

HOLY. Shit.

"We waited a fucking hour in this line, and it's going to be over in less than five minutes?" Phoenix asks with a bite to his tone. It's also trembling, and I briefly wonder if he's afraid of heights. He glares when I laugh, but he can't see me once he slides into his own seat behind me and Raven.

I don't know what I did to get her next to me with Pierce and Phoenix behind us, but I'm grateful. Even if we are at the very front.

I think my girl has a love of danger if the bright smile and crazed look in her eyes are anything to go by.

"You're fucking crazy," I tell her as I strap myself in.

She grins in my direction, and my heart hammers in my chest.

I need to fucking tell her. Now. Before I chicken out.

Pierce is going to scream like a little girl, she signs, then tries to peer over her shoulder at the man in question, but can't because of the size of the bucket seat we're in.

"I don't know what she just said, but she's lying," Pierce yells from behind me, and I chuckle in response.

The attendant goes over all the rules, then talks a bit about the history of the ride and how it's one of the few classics left on site. He then tells us it'll shoot us out at the top at high speeds and won't slow down until the very end, so we need to take a breath now before it begins. He wishes us good luck before pressing a button, and we creep upwards at a painstakingly slow pace.

Into a tunnel.

Fuck, I don't know how I feel about this anymore.

Rae reaches over and grabs my hand, sliding her fingers between mine and resting our hands between our two seats. The brightest smile lights up her face when I meet her eyes, and I swear I wish like hell we were on solid ground.

Maybe telling her here won't be so bad. She's happy, in a great mood actually, and I could yell it from the top of the coaster and it would be like yelling it from the rooftops.

She deserves to have this fantastic day to remember.

As we creep toward the top, I grip her hand tighter. "Hey, RaeRae?"

She looks back over at me and tilts her head to the side in question.

"There's something I want to tell you, sweet girl. I think now is a great time because you'll remember it forever like this. And honestly, I want everything to be memorable for you. Everything. Even the small moments should be remarkable for you. Life has sucked for a long time without you. You've made every small and big moment since I've met you something incredible and—"

The coaster pulls back, my gut clenches, and I can no longer speak as we're thrust outward and spit onto what turns out to be the wildest ride of my life.

Despite the fact that I didn't get to tell Raven Hill that I'm in love with her.

RAERAE

Hey Riv?

What's up?

RAERAE

I'm really worried about Nix. He's so closed off. He won't tell me much, either. I just... I'm worried.

I've been worried since he went to see the guy in jail.

RAERAE

Is Pierce finding anything else out?

Not much. Nixy boy is trying to keep up to date and he's feeling a little guilty that he left his old friends behind.

Also, he's torn up over not going to the funeral.

RAERAE

Why would he want to go to her fucking funeral?

I don't know, baby. You said it before. They did love each other a shit ton when they were together.

RAERAE

Do you think if it wasn't for her father that they'd still be together?

Nah. You'd have still come along and swept him off his feet.

RAERAE

I can't compare to that type of eternal and unconditional love, Riv.

I think you'd be surprised. Take a breath, baby. He'll be right as rain ASAP. I swear it.

raven

"I'm never going to an amusement park with you ever again. Ever, River," Phoenix says, glaring at River like he was the only one who wanted to go on the coaster to begin with.

River grins and wraps his arm around Phoenix's shoulder, kissing the top of his head as quickly as he can before he's pushed away.

I shake my head, laughing at their antics as we walk toward the park entrance. Before the boys can get too rowdy, I grab River's hand and tug him to a standstill. With shaking hands, I sign, *What were you going to tell me at the top of the coaster?*

River's eyes widen, and he swallows before shaking his head and plastering a fake grin on his face. "Nothing important right now, RaeRae. Let's head back to the hotel and get some relaxing in before we meet this Riley dude tomorrow. Okay?"

He doesn't wait for me to answer before he wraps his

arm around my shoulders and tugs me to his side. We stride forward quickly to catch up with the other guys.

I swear he was going to tell me he loved me. Either he chickened out or he didn't have the chance to say it because of the way he was rambling just before the coaster sent us over the edge. A smile spreads across my lips as I rest my head against River's shoulder and breathe him in.

We leave the fun of our trip behind and prepare to meet someone who very well could become another name on our list of enemies.

When we climb into the cab on the way back to our hotel, Pierce pulls me to sit between him and River and places his hand on my knee. He looks over at me with a bright smile, windswept hair, and eyes lit with happiness. Before I can manage any reaction, he leans forward and kisses me, then continues well past the point when the driver clears his throat and Phoenix snaps at us to stop.

River wastes no time when we get to the hotel, either. He pulls me from the cab and tosses me over his shoulder, slapping me on the thigh when I try to wiggle free.

We're a sight to see, but unfortunately for me, Phoenix gets lost in his phone again the entire way to the elevator, down the hall, and into our room.

I've never been this truly frustrated with him, and I have no idea what to do about it.

The choice is taken from me when River brings me into the bathroom, places me on the counter, and starts up the jacuzzi tub.

"Hey!" Pierce shouts. "I better be included in that bath or we're gonna have problems, River."

"Untwist your panties, Piercey Jackson. You're both invited to this party, too." River leans over me, forcing me backward until his mouth is level with my chest. He grins wickedly before placing soft kisses along my exposed collarbone.

I've never been more thankful for shorts and a tank top in my life.

I squirm under his soft touches and kisses until I'm soaked, and I can feel the weight of his hardness against my leg as he leans against me.

"Strip and get in the tub, little vixen." River backs away and undresses himself.

Pierce enters the room with some fresh towels and leans against the doorframe and watches as River and I strip naked. He places the towels down on the counter where I was sitting, then reaches behind himself to pull his shirt up over his head. River laughs when the shirt lands on his head.

I inhale sharply as he strips his pants and boxers off, chewing my lip as I take in how hard he is. My gaze flashes to the doorway, but River grips my chin and kisses me until my worries for Phoenix are pushed to the back of my mind.

"Don't worry about him, little bird," Pierce says in my ear. He nips my earlobe and pulls it between his teeth before sliding up behind me. He kisses a path down my neck as River releases me and does the same to the other side. "We're going to make you feel so good. You won't have to worry about a damn thing."

River chuckles darkly, and I squirm between them, lifting my hands to clutch at his biceps. "You won't have the power to worry. We'll make your brain blitz from the orgasms we give you." He grips my chin again and brings my gaze to meet his. "That good with you, Rae?"

I nod a few times and he grins before picking me up around the back of my thighs to carry me to the tub. The heat of the water and the massage from the jets help my body relax. Not even the smell of basic hotel soap can dissuade me from relaxing in this jacuzzi right now.

River and Pierce climb in, and the water sloshes over the side, but they pay it no mind. They work together to move my body between them; feet in River's lap while my back is against Pierce's chest.

What a fucking dream.

If only Phoenix were to find a way to participate.

Is he okay? I sign, hoping one of them is honest with me. I know they've each had a conversation with Phoenix, and I'm the only one left out of the loop.

Pierce sighs and massages my shoulders and neck muscles, kneading the tension from the various thrill rides today.

River looks up as he starts to rub my aching feet, and I toss my head back on Pierce's shoulder, keeping my eyes on River's. His jaw tenses, and the way his body moves as stiff as it does points out his stress level, but he breaks into that fake smile again.

I'm half tempted to kick him in the face for trying to hide from me.

"Phoenix is…" Pierce says, but River speaks up and interrupts him as his smile fades into a frown.

"He's fucked up about Lexi, Rae. At one point, he really loved her, so having her gone like this is a completely different feeling than if she were in prison getting help." River clutches my foot a little too tight, apologizing when I wince. He shakes his head and continues. "I hate the fact that he's mourning her, but he is, so that's just something we have to help him through."

Who the hell is he texting this whole time? I sign. That's been my biggest worry, because I thought he was done with everyone from his old life. Only, I see him texting and calling people at all hours of the day. I feel like I don't know enough about what's happening.

"He's talking a lot to his old band mates. They all had a falling out after Lexi killed his family. He left everyone behind. But they've been keeping him updated on everything. Checking up on him. He's been telling one of them about you, though. He was texting pictures of our day to them." River meets my gaze and smiles, head tilted to the side as he moves his hand up my calf. "Don't worry, Rae. He'll be fine once this whole bullshit part of his life is put to rest."

"Literally," Pierce snarks. "Lexi's funeral is tomorrow."

"And we'll be too distracted meeting with Mark Riley to give a damn." River slides one hand away from me, running it up Pierce's leg instead, and the visual ignites a fire in my body.

I bite my lip and squirm in Pierce's hold, my lower back rubbing against his cock until I feel him harden against me. My eyes meet River's, and he looks between Pierce and me before getting on all fours and crawling toward us as best he can in the tub.

"Let us be enough for you tonight, little vixen. Please?" he asks, sitting back on his haunches once he's between mine and Pierce's legs. He rests one hand on my leg and the other on Pierce's, then scratches his fingernails up along our skin.

We both shiver, and Pierce groans in response, bucking his hips forward so his dick slides against me.

I nod once, and River descends like a madman, kissing and thrusting his tongue into my mouth. He reaches between us and massages one breast, then the other, and slides his hand down between my legs to thrust two fingers inside of me.

My hips surge upwards, and I break from the kiss to let out a breath, squeezing my eyes shut tight against the welcomed invasion. Despite the water, I know I'm wet all on my own, and by the way River's fingers glide in and out of me, I'm right.

"Fuck, you're so beautiful," Pierce whispers in my ear. He slides his hands between me and River, pinching my nipple in one hand, and using the other to stroke River's cock.

I think I die in this moment. There's no way in hell I'm sandwiched between these two as they explore me and each other.

It's too fucking much.

I grind my clit against River's palm as he thrusts his fingers into me, and when he leans forward to kiss Pierce instead of me, I come so hard and fast I'll forever wonder if it really happened.

They both chuckle as they break from their kiss, and Pierce nips at my neck as River pulls back to look down at me with a filthy grin.

"Do you like us together like this, little vixen?" River asks, bucking his hips upward to slide his dick through Pierce's fist.

I watch them and nod, sure at this point I'm drooling.

"Filthy little bird," Pierce groans in my ear. He pumps his fist over River faster until he reaches down and grabs Pierce's hand, stilling it and reluctantly pulling away.

"I'm getting a damn cramp. Let's get out and head to bed." River climbs out of the tub and reaches for my hand.

As I stand, Pierce places a loud kiss on my ass cheek. I

toss my head back on a laugh, then look back to smile at him.

"Don't even think about making a comment. Your ass is too much of a temptation." He stands up and slaps each of my cheeks before wrapping a towel around my wet body and ushering me out of the room.

Phoenix is on the phone, but when he sees us entering completely naked aside from the towels, he hangs up and rakes his heated gaze from my head to my toes and back again.

I shiver and bite my lip, watching as he walks forward and begins to strip himself like a man possessed.

He doesn't care that he breaks the buttons on his shirt, and instead of being neat like he always is, he tosses his clothes haphazardly around the room as he makes his way toward me. The moment he's standing naked in front of me, he collars my throat and kisses me.

I reach up and slide my hands through his hair, tugging at the bun on his head before letting it loose. He groans as I massage his scalp, then pushes me until the back of my thighs hit the mattress. I laugh as I fall backward, meeting all three of the guys' heated gazes as they surround the bed.

"You want us to fuck the stress out of you, Red?" Phoenix asks.

My breathing speeds up and my heart hammers in my chest at the dark tone in his voice.

I nod, tap the mattress once to confirm my out, then sign, *Green.*

I want them to screw my brains out ruthlessly.

If only to get me out of my head.

Phoenix grabs the guys by the shoulder and takes them to a corner of the room. They whisper and conspire amongst themselves for a few minutes before turning back to me with a wicked gleam in their eyes.

I'm so fucked.

Thank Satan.

Phoenix is the first to approach. The bed dips as he climbs onto it and kisses me again until I'm left panting, breathless, and soaked. He maneuvers himself beneath me and holds out his hand. River places a bottle of lube in his hand and I watch as he coats his shaft in it before grabbing me and plastering my back to his chest. He nips my ear. "Relax, Red." He groans as he slides his dick into my ass slowly, the strain in his shaking legs the only visible tell he gives of his frustration. Slowly, he pumps in and out of me until he can thrust all the way inside. "Shit," he whispers, biting down on my shoulder as he stills.

Pierce climbs onto the bed next, and as he positions himself between mine and Phoenix's thighs, I get a real visual for what they have planned. He slides a finger through my wet folds, grinning and bringing it to his mouth to suck before positioning himself at my entrance. He leans down and kisses me as he enters me, and my entire body tenses under the stretch and fullness he and Phoenix put me through.

"You doing okay, little bird?" Pierce asks. I nod, and he groans as he forces himself to still. "Unclench, baby, or Nix and I are gonna blow faster than we want."

I relax, taking deep breaths as I get used to this fullness again. This has nothing on Valentine's Day, because River climbs on the bed behind Pierce, reaches for the lube, and winks at me. I clench around Pierce's cock and he groans in my ear, biting down on my earlobe as he holds himself up on shaking hands.

"Hurry the fuck up," Phoenix snaps, his voice strained.

"Hear that, pup?" River snarks at Pierce, placing a hand in his hair. He pulls Pierce's face up and I watch as they kiss for a moment. "He says we need to hurry. Are you ready for me?"

Pierce's eyes meet mine before he nods, his entire body seizing up on him a moment later.

"I didn't hear you," River says, and Pierce is thrust forward, his dick burying deeper inside of me.

"Yes, master," Pierce grits out, embarrassment turning his cheeks pink.

"Good boy," River says, grinning until his face becomes one of concentration.

I grip Pierce's shoulders as River slides his dick inside of him, and my jaw drops with fascination as I watch the gentle yet rough way they handle each other.

Once River fully seats himself inside of Pierce, the entire group takes a collective breath, and I can't help but let out a small huff of laughter. Unfortunately, it makes me clench around Pierce, and he glares down at me as a vein in his forehead bulges.

"Seems our little vixen thinks this is funny," River says. He grins at me, then leans forward and thrusts inside of Pierce roughly enough that my whole body lights with pleasure. "Not so funny now, is it Rae?"

I shake my head and rest against Phoenix, allowing the boys to manipulate me as they slowly move with each other, creating a symphony of sensation in my body. This has nothing on Valentine's Day, because I get to watch the love Pierce and River share with each other. The trust.

Phoenix's body slides against mine, and he alternates

between kissing my neck and biting it, no doubt leaving his mark on my skin.

Pierce reaches between us and circles my clit, groaning when I clench around him in response. "Fuck," he breathes, leaning down to kiss me. He thrusts his tongue into my mouth and devours me as they pick up their pace, invading my body as much as my heart and soul when they do.

The sounds of skin slapping skin, rough grunts, and moans fill the hotel room. I'm sure we're a sight to fucking behold. I close my eyes against the onslaught of emotion and allow myself to feel more.

"Jesus Christ," Phoenix whispers. He moans as his hips stutter. "Fuck. Come for us Red. I can't come until you do. So fucking come. Do you hear me?"

I nod enough times that I become dizzy, and Pierce doubles his efforts, thrusting into me at just the right angle to drag along my g-spot as he massages my clit.

River reaches between us and pinches one of my nipples, and when he thrusts inside of Pierce, everything is hit at once and I'm sent soaring into oblivion, careening over a waterfall, gushing over Pierce and Phoenix as my soul leaves my fucking body.

Phoenix comes with a guttural moan, cinching his arm around my waist as he thrusts until he's spent. Pierce finishes seconds later, with River following right behind with a pained shout.

You'd think we'd all lay here and catch our breath, but Phoenix says something about cum leaking onto him, and Pierce and River laugh obnoxiously as they pull away and head to the shower.

Phoenix grabs me and cleans me up in the shower when they're done, then he helps me into one of his old band t-shirts, something I didn't even know he brought with him. He admires it for a moment before bringing me in for a surprisingly tender hug and kissing the top of my head.

"I'm sorry I've been so fucking absent on this trip. I promise I'll put it all away for the rest of the time we have, okay?" He pulls back and holds my face in his hands, looking down at me so sweetly my heart melts. "I love you," he whispers, almost as if he's still scared to say it.

I mouth the words back to him, and he kisses me before wrapping me in his arms and walking me to the freshly made bed.

Warmth encapsulates me as I curl up between River and Phoenix. Then I yawn for so long they all end up yawning too, with loud complaints that I'm making them tired. As if they didn't just rail me into a half-coma. I close my eyes and push all thoughts of tomorrow away as the room quiets and we all find the rest we need.

phoenix

Rae's soft snores are quiet when she rolls over and smothers herself with her pillow like usual. Watching her sleep so soundly settles something in my chest, and I'm glad we could help her fall into a trance like that.

I smile and shake my head before kissing her cheek and climbing out of the bed to go take a piss.

This trip should have been fun, even if our destination would not be. It's a damn shame I had to spend most of it reminiscing with my old friends instead of focusing on them.

My family.

After washing my hands, I take a deep breath and am about to climb onto the bed when I notice Pierce missing, followed by a flicker of light coming from the balcony. I grab my phone and head out there, quietly opening and closing the door.

He's looking down at his own screen with a furrowed

brow, and has a cigarette between his lips. He's stress smoking.

What the fuck happened now?

"You know Red hates it when you smoke, right?" I ask him, and bite back my cocky grin when he jumps.

He tosses the ashes over the railing and sticks it between his lips again. He takes a long drag and nods. "I know."

I walk forward and steal the cigarette from him, inhaling deeply and blowing it out before passing it back. "Why are we smoking?"

He shakes his head and takes another drag from the smoke before answering. "I really don't want to air my dirty laundry to Starling. I don't trust him."

"Eventually, you have to trust someone."

"I trust you three, and that's good enough." He looks down at his phone and types out a reply to a text.

"What's Lance doing up so late?" I ask, taking the cigarette back when it's offered.

"Thinks he saw Jimmy fucking Perkins at the park today."

"The fuck?" I pass the smoke back and go to sit in a plastic chair. "This is bullshit. How do we keep her safe if Maxwell is fucking everywhere?"

Pierce puts the cigarette out and tosses the remains over the railing before sitting next to me. "Dunno man. I have no fucking clue."

"Hence the stress smoking," I say with a raised brow in his direction.

"Hence the fucking stress smoking."

We're quiet for a few minutes, then my phone lights up. Though I told myself I'd ignore it until I absolutely needed it again, I pick it up and click into Ryan's message.

RYAN

WTF?

A link to a news article follows his message, and when I open it, my mouth drops wide open.

"What the fuck?" I whisper.

Xavier Hayes Pleads Guilty to Murder of ex-girl-friend, Alexis Sommers

Xavier Hayes has been held in the county jail for weeks now under the allegations that he murdered his girlfriend over an argument they had about his increasing drug use.

The trial was due to start next week after a week of back and forth with authorities. The Sommers family sought attorneys to charge Hayes with this heinous crime, but barely three days before the trial was due to start, Hayes pled guilty.

He will serve 40 years in a state penitentiary, which is lucky, because a trial could have placed him there for life. Unfortunately for Hayes, the Sommers family is deeply unsettled by this outcome and they are pleading with the state to extend his sentence.

Only time will tell what will happen, but at the end of the day, he still committed a crime of the sickest variety.

Whitaker Sommers asks that the press allow the family time to properly grieve Alexis, and that all donations be made to his church to help other lost youth in their community.

You can find information below on how to donate.

What. The. Fuck.

"Well," Pierce says with a laugh. "Serves the fucker right for what he did to you on New Year's Eve."

"He didn't fucking do this," I snap, bouncing back to my message thread with Ryan.

> He didn't fucking do this. I met with him, and he didn't fucking do this.

RYAN

> What do you mean you met with him? Why the fuck would you meet with the guy?

Shit, shit, shit.

I press the button to call him and tap my foot as I wait for him to answer.

He yawns as he picks up. "What the fuck, Nix? It's late."

"It's eleven over there, Ryan. I'm not an idiot with time zones."

"Yeah, but it's what... two... three in the morning?" He sighs. "Why did you go visit him, Nix?"

"He beat the fuck out of me on New Year's Eve. Was defending her."

"The hell... what? What kind of shit are you lost in, man?"

I run a hand through my hair and grab the cigarette from

Pierce's hand, noticing my fingers trembling. He helps me light it and I take a drag before speaking again. "Don't worry about it. How do we get help for this guy? There's no fucking way he killed her."

"I dunno, Nix. Let me think on it and I'll call you back tomorrow, okay?"

"You can't!" I shout, then wince and look back inside the hotel room to make sure I didn't wake Raven. "You can't call me tomorrow. I have important things going on. Find this guy some help. He needs it, okay? I won't be back in the state until next week, so whatever you can do to help him, please do, okay? This has Whitaker's name all fucking over it."

"Calm the hell down, Nix," Pierce tells me, snatching the cigarette from my hand. It was about to burn my fingers.

"Nix—"

"I... I'm sorry Ryan. I'll call you sometime next week, okay?" I don't wait for him to respond. I simply hang up on him and walk toward the railing of the balcony, staring out at the rest of the city.

It's quiet for a few minutes, then Pierce walks up to my side and pats my shoulder, sighing when I flinch.

"You're coming unhinged over this. Over everything. I need you to have a clear fucking head for tomorrow, especially if we end up with the recipe."

I sigh and rest my head on my forearms, closing my eyes as I take deep breaths.

It's quiet for a few minutes and Pierce says nothing as he allows me the time to process this information.

When it's clear I'm not planning to move soon, he pulls me away from the railing. "Let's go get some fucking sleep, yeah?"

I walk with him, my whole body numb as I process everything that's going on.

Or fail to process it, anyway.

As I climb into bed, Raven curls into my side and places her head on my chest. I inhale her sweet strawberry soda scent, barely there from using the various hotel soaps over the past week, and allow my brain to shut the fuck up so I can sleep.

RIV

You enjoying your little cuddle back there?

You salty, Jacobs?

RIV

Fuck. Don't call me that. And yes. Yes, I am
feeling salty.

gif of a salt shaker

Should have won, then. *shrug emoji*

RIV

Cold, baby.

Pierce used to want to drag race when we
were in high school.

RIV

Did he?

Fuck no. I was too scared he'd die, so I
told him not to.

RIV

But you're the one who encouraged it
tonight... I'm confused.

Sometimes... when we put limitations on
those we love... we hurt them more often
than not.

So instead of telling him I don't want him to
die, I encouraged him to win. Winning
should = not dying.

RIV

You're the greatest girlfriend alive, RaeRae.

Too soon for that joke, Riv. Too fucking
soon.

RIV

If I give you another bag of Twirlers will you forgive me?

Maybe.

raven

"That's everything," Pierce says, closing the trunk of the rental. He looks up at the hotel and blows out a long breath before looking down at me.

Why do you look so sad? I sign.

He shrugs, walks toward me, and pulls me into his arms. His hand cradles my head against his chest as he breathes me in.

The sense of immense dread strengthens as we near the end of this trip, and get closer to meeting Mark Riley.

Not one of us is sure what we'll find when we meet him, and the reception could go from hesitant to full on hostile. It's the latter we're all truly afraid of, especially if he's still somehow connected to my father.

God only knows we don't need Maxwell up our asses.

I open my eyes to study our surroundings again. The feeling of being watched has grown stronger over the last two days. The amusement park was one thing, and I could explain that away with Lance and his guys spread around us at all times. But this...

Pierce places his finger beneath my chin and lifts it until our mouths meet. A sweet and desperate kiss meant to calm me, but only sets off more alarm bells.

"All checked out and ready to go," River calls as he walks out of the hotel, the last bag slung over his shoulder.

I meet his gaze and smile as I walk toward the front seat and climb into the car. As the boys get in one by one, I take a deep breath.

Phoenix hops in last. He's glued to his phone, though his eyes are so heavy lidded I wonder if he can see the thing. He looks up in time to meet my gaze. *I'm fine, Red*, he signs, then yawns and leans his head back on his seat.

"You know what we can do for two hours, RaeRae?" River leans between the seats, his grin wide and eyes sparkling with mischief.

"If you say I Spy again, I'm going to get you a booster seat and shut you up with a pacifier in your mouth, River." Pierce slams his door shut, then turns his head to stare our golden retriever down.

River barks out a laugh, kisses my cheek, then Pierce's, and sits back in his seat with a shake of his head. "I'll get you back for that, pup. Show you what you can use as a pacifier real fuckin' quick to stop your tantrum, yeah?"

Phoenix laughs at that one, and I cover my mouth to hide my own, then turn my head to watch out the window as we pull out of the parking lot.

"THIS... CAN'T BE RIGHT." Pierce leans over the steering wheel as he stares through the windshield.

"I mean, he's done good for himself." River leans forward, trying to get a better view. "You think he's like an accountant or something now? Something normal and not... you know... kill a whole town with drugs type?"

I doubt a simple accountant would have a house like this, I sign.

"Yeah, you're right." River sits back in his seat and looks at Pierce. "We going in?"

Pierce glances over at me with eyes full of worry and doubt. "Can I convince you to stay in the car, Blue? At all? For us to find out what kind of bullshit we are walking into?"

I shake my head once, unlock my door, climb out, and slam it shut behind me. I'm becoming increasingly irritated with these men and them telling me what the fuck to do. They can worry their little hearts out, but I'm not a goddamn damsel in distress.

"Raven," Phoenix snaps as he climbs out of the car.

I pay him no fucking mind. Gravel crunches beneath my feet as I walk toward the front steps of the brick mini-mansion Mark Riley calls home. How Maxwell hasn't found this guy is a question for the ages, because he's drawing attention to himself.

Or maybe that's the red herring of it all.

The only way to tell is to meet him and find out what the hell he's been doing for the last nineteen years.

The black double front door sparkles in the morning light, and as I reach forward to grab the brass knocker, a slight breeze catches my hair and whips it behind me. I shiver, and dread grows in my gut as I take another look behind me.

The boys argue between themselves until they ultimately decide to shove Pierce in the firing line. He makes his way toward my side and places his hand on my lower back and lets out a long breath before meeting my eyes. He nods once and straightens his shoulders. Preparing himself for the worst.

What even is the worst?

I lift the handle and knock once.

Twice.

Three times.

Then take a step back and try to maintain my composure with my hands at my sides and eyes straight ahead, portraying all the false confidence I can muster.

One door opens with a loud creak, dust falling from between the cracks, and I'm met with the prettiest hazel eyes I've seen in a long time. A woman who looks to be about our age steps forward, but immediately moves back and exhales a shaky breath. "I-I'm sorry. I have no idea who you are. We haven't had visitors in—"

"Beatrice! I told you never to answer the door," a male booms from behind her.

She flinches back, then pushes the door in an attempt to close it with an apologetic and panicked expression on her face.

Pierce shoves his foot in the doorway, and the wood ricochets off his combat boot and opens wider as the woman continues to take steps backward.

"Beatrice," the man shouts again, this time from much, much closer. "I thought I told you to—"

He appears in the doorway then, his dark eyes wide, gray hair tousled and stretching in all directions. He stops speaking when he sees us, then grabs the woman and shoves her to stand behind him.

She stumbles, clutching onto him to keep herself upright before letting go as if his skin burns her alive.

I narrow my eyes on Mark Riley before looking back at those hazel eyes, trying to get a feel for who she is and if she needs our help.

She helps nothing when she hides behind him further, keeping herself hidden from us.

Mark Riley continues to stare at us. Me, specifically. The silence stretches until he bolts forward, grabs the door, and tries to slam it so hard I hear Pierce hiss through his teeth as it slams against his boot again.

The door swings wide open this time, bouncing off the wall, and Pierce takes a step into the dark foyer. This place no doubt hides more secrets than Riley is willing to part with.

"No. She's his daughter. Nope. Beatrice, go pack your bags. The day has come for us to leave, my love." He turns and grabs her shoulders and hustles her down the hall. He looks back over his shoulder at us, gasping when River and Phoenix walk in. "Please leave us alone! We've done nothing wrong! Two decades. Nothing wrong. Nope. Nothing." He walks into another room and slams the door shut.

Pierce wiggles the handle and growls when he finds it locked. "Mark Riley, we're only here to talk to you."

"I know who she belongs to, young man!" Riley shouts from the other side of the door.

"This just got extremely complicated." River sighs as he steps up beside me and tosses an arm over my shoulders.

Phoenix moves to Pierce's side and they both work to get the door unlocked. "What now?" he asks.

"We get this door open, grab him, tie him down, and get him to talk." Pierce puts a hand on Phoenix's shoulder, and they both take a step back. His shoulders rise and fall before he rushes forward and shoves his boot hard enough at the door that it splinters when it opens.

Mark Riley stands in the center of the room with a suit-case full of paperwork, and when my boys walk inside, he tries to close it. He isn't fast enough, and all three descend on him, grabbing his arms as they plaster him to an armchair.

Phoenix pulls a coil of rope from his back pocket and begins tying Riley up to the chair as River walks toward the scared woman named Beatrice in the corner.

I make a split second decision I'm sure I'll never hear the end of. I place my hand on River's chest and push him back a step, then turn toward the woman and take careful steps toward her. Meeting her tear-filled eyes, I hold a hand up as if to show her I mean her no harm.

She still flinches, curling in on herself and taking rapid breaths. "I-I-I... I haven't... we haven't done an-anything! P-Please just leave us alone!" she screeches, tears falling like a waterfall down her cheeks.

River moves to my side and holds his hands up as he approaches her. "I don't want to hurt you. I never would. We just want to ask him some questions. See if he can help us. Sit with my girl here?" He points toward me, but keeps his gaze on her.

After a few measured breaths, she looks over my shoulder at the state of her father, then looks back at me and River and nods.

"Good. Sit on the couch there, and we won't have to tie you up, too. Okay?" River's voice is soothing, and it gets the job done because she walks forward and takes a seat.

I follow, then swallow back my own nerves when I sit

next to her and watch Pierce glare down at Mark Riley as if he's the reason for all our problems.

I mean, he kind of is, but he's not the mastermind.

From the terrified look in his eyes, it seems he was just a pawn in Maxwell's games as much as we are.

"You know," Pierce says, his voice haunting and dark. "You treated my girl rudely back there. I should knock your fucking teeth out for it."

"Please!" Riley shouts. He wiggles, shakes, moves, all to try and get free.

"I think he needs to say sorry," River says as he steps behind the chair. He grabs Riley's head and makes him stare directly at me. "Apologize and I won't let my pup here have his way with you."

Riley relaxes his shoulders and blows out a breath.

River chuckles. "At least not yet, anyway."

Riley twists and turns, yelling and shouting as River holds his head.

"So, apologize for being so rude to Raven, Mark Riley." River's personality shift makes me question everything I've learned about these men in the past six months.

I realize I've kept them distracted, and that they've done a lot of seedy shit for Maxwell... but this? This is unsettling, dark, demented... and I'm only a little frustrated that it turns me on.

"Well?" Pierce asks, leaning down into Riley's face. "Are you going to apologize for being rude to our girl? The consequences for not doing so could be..."

"Dire," River finishes for him, laughing when Riley flinches, almost as if he'd forgotten River existed for a moment.

With his head held firm, Riley's dark eyes land on me,

and my entire body freezes. His eyes are lifeless, like the man has seen too much. Done too much. He inhales sharply before speaking. "I apologize."

It's so insincere, but Pierce smacks his cheek before standing and indicating River should release him.

"Can we get on with this?" Phoenix asks, exasperated.

Beatrice curls up in the corner of the couch, keeping her eyes firmly on her father.

"W-What do you want to know? W-Why are you here?" he asks.

"Well, it seems you recognize our lovely little bird over there, so I'm sure you have assumptions about who we are and why we're here." Pierce grins and puts his hands in his pockets as he stands in front of Riley. "Tell us what you think you know first. We'll tell you if you're wrong."

"Maybe," River adds.

"You two are annoying," Phoenix says with a sigh as he sits on the coffee table in front of Riley, pushing Pierce off to the side. "We're running out of time here, Mark. I hope I can call you Mark. Anyway, we're here for you to make an anti-drug for Rapture."

Riley barks out a quick laugh and shakes his head, amusement clear in his tone when he speaks. "That fucking drug got out again, didn't it? Where was the recipe? I bet it was with his bitch of a sister. She always hated him."

"Shut the fuck up," Pierce snaps. "That's my girl's mother you're talking about."

"Mother? Everlyn never had kids." Riley stares at me with a creased brow. "No. You're the spitting image of Maxwell and Priscilla. They had to have made you in a lab with how perfect you match them."

"I said," Pierce growls as he leans toward Riley. "Shut.

The. Fuck. Up." He reaches into his jeans and grabs a pocket knife, holding it up to the man's throat.

"I bet she loves that you talk for her. Not even letting her speak for herself." Riley laughs when Pierce knicks him, and Beatrice squeals. She rushes toward him, but I stretch my arm out to hold her back.

"She suffers from traumatic mutism," Phoenix explains. "Not like it's any of your business."

"Well, that's tragic," Riley says. He laughs again, high pitched, unhinged, terrified.

"Daddy, please," Beatrice whines from my side. She curls back into a ball and looks around. I'm not sure if she's scared *of him* or *for him* at this point. Her behavior is erratic, and as I watch her pull her stringy brown hair into a knot at the top of her head, I wonder if she's conditioned to care for him. If she actually is his daughter, or if he stole her.

"Okay, Riley," Pierce says. He stands to his full height and folds his arms over his chest. "You aren't leaving. She's not leaving. You're going to tell us everything, then you'll help us with an anti-drug because your recipe is out there killing people."

"Again," River adds.

"I'm not saying shit when I'm tied up like this," Riley snarls.

"Fair enough," Pierce says. Riley's eyes widen in surprise when Phoenix walks around the chair and unties him. "Make a wrong move and you'll end up back in the chair with a few new scars, though."

Riley nods and looks over to Beatrice for a fleeting moment while he's being untied. When he's free, he brings his hands into his lap and massages the spots the rope dug into. "Beatrice, why don't you go get our... guests... some tea?"

"Nope," Pierce says, pointing at her. "Do not move." He glares back at Riley as he takes a seat next to Phoenix on the table. "Start fucking talking."

Riley scratches his neck and looks around at all of the guys before sighing in defeat and leaning back into the chair. When his eyes glaze over, I wonder if he's dissociating and is about to ignore us, but he blows out a long breath, and I get the feeling that we're in for a story.

"Maxwell Langston in the late nineties was the most charismatic man I've ever met," Riley begins. "He grabbed us in his clutches and never really let any of us go. We formed a bond, him and I, and when he talked about creating our fraternity, Alpha Mu—"

"Yeah, we know that," Pierce says. "He made Alpha Mu and ran a drug ring, hoping to continue it and keep making money from it for the rest of his life. What we need you to tell us is who the fuck else is involved, why you got pulled in, and how to make a proper anti-drug to this, because you're our only source of help. You created this, so it's now your responsibility to fucking fix it."

Riley stares at Pierce for a moment, then nods once and looks down at his hands. "Maxwell introduced me to my wife, Holly, mid-way through the creation of Rapture. We were inseparable to the point she would wait outside the Alpha Mu house anytime I had a meeting. She made some other friends. Chloe, Priscilla, and Melissa. A few years into it, she made friends with Everlyn, too. Those girls were always attached at the hip." Mark smiles as if he can see the memories clear as day, but then he frowns. "Maxwell wanted to test it on them first, but Holly and Everlyn refused."

"But the others... they survived it," River says, brows furrowed.

Riley nods. "The first dose wasn't as strong, and we barely let them take half of one. The effect we were going for was almost immediate. They were basking in euphoria. Turned on, energetic, seeking more. After about six hours, when they were still going, I got worried. I'd never seen a drug last that long without an added dose." He sighs and shakes his head. "When Maxwell saw the benefit of a long-lasting drug like this, he decided it was time to use it. That's all we had to do before we put it out in the world."

"You only tested a small portion of a dose... then just went ahead and put full doses out there?" Phoenix asks in surprise.

"Unfortunately," Riley says. "I tried to get him to wait. To test more, but he wouldn't. Holly and Everlyn stopped hanging around the house entirely, and my relationship became strained. Holly became pregnant shortly after, and the further along she got, the more angry she turned. It was as if her instincts were screaming at her to leave. She said she would if I continued, and she did... for a while, at least." He takes a deep breath and buries his face in his hands. After a moment of gathering himself, he looks back at the guys again. "Maxwell... he said he'd take her from me if I didn't help him. So... I kept helping."

"Why didn't you report him?" Pierce asks. "All you had to do was go to the police."

"Whitaker Sommers and Robert Jacobs strong-armed me into staying. Whitaker would take photos of Holly, threaten me with her. Robert... well, he had connections with people who could make her disappear." Riley looks over at his daughter. "I only wanted to protect you both. So I stayed." He turns his gaze back to the guys. "I kept my head down and kept working. I made excuse after excuse about things going wrong until Maxwell locked me into the science wing one weekend until I produced enough for one of our frat parties. Three days later... five people were dead."

"What did Maxwell do when the people died?" Phoenix asks.

I clutch my hands in my lap as I take in all the information, and my heart damn near stops working as I wait for his next words.

"Beat the hell out of me. Cut one of my toes off." Riley winces at the memory. "I told Holly to pack her bags.... and we left the next day. I have no idea what happened after that. Maxwell had a daughter in the hospital with Priscilla, and I know Chloe had her baby the day after."

"Wait," River says. "Priscilla and Chloe were both pregnant... and they still tried this drug?" He shakes his head. "That's disgusting."

"They'd been on drugs for years, and they thought they were invincible. I felt the worst about Melissa. She already had an infant, but she left him at home while she came around. Whitaker and his wife had a toddler. Dexter, I believe they named him. They were seniors at the time, but had connections in town with the police, so we flew so far under the radar, it was as if we never existed to them outside of school."

River takes a deep breath and storms out of the room. The front door opens and closes loudly, and I flinch before looking at Pierce in question.

He glares at Mark, then glances at Phoenix. "Have this

guy teach you everything we need to know." He shifts his gaze to me and points to Beatrice. "Keep her company, please? I don't want her running off and calling the cops."

"We can't," Riley says with a laugh.

"What?" Pierce asks, turning back to glare at him.

"We can't call the police. This entire property is off grid. Even your cells won't work." Riley laughs again, then grunts when Pierce punches him in the gut. "You fuck!"

"Don't make me put a muzzle on you, Riley. Be a good boy for Nix here and we'll be on our way as soon as humanly fucking possible." Pierce leans down to kiss my cheek as he leaves the room, and I watch him disappear down the hallway.

What's going on? I sign to Phoenix.

Melissa is his mom, he signs back before turning to Riley and pointing at the suitcase.

I look toward the hallway, wishing I could soothe the acute pain River must be in, but before I can, Beatrice shifts in her seat and I pin her to the spot with a glare.

Guess I'm stuck babysitting...

pierce

"**R**iver!" I shout as I exit the house. I can't see him anywhere.

I walk around the car, open the doors, and search the trunk like a fucking idiot. Panicked, I pull my phone from my pocket. But as I dial his number, I freeze when I notice the lack of service. Riley said we're blocked out here. Guess he was telling the truth.

"Riv! Man, come on." I run a hand through my hair and walk to one side of the house, keeping my eyes peeled for any movement.

Halfway around the back, there's a gate that I have to kick with my boot to get open, and when I do, I find him sitting on a lounge chair in front of an empty in-ground pool. His shoulders are shaking.

From sadness... or rage?

"River," I call his name again, quieter this time.

He doesn't move.

I take a few steps toward him and sit on the chair closest

to his. After a few seconds, I lean my elbows on my knees and raise my eyes to meet his.

His are red-rimmed from the tears falling down his cheeks, and my heart sinks in my chest when he clenches and unclenches his fists at his sides. He closes his eyes and shakes his head. "Leave me alone for like... a good hour, yeah?"

While swallowing all the pride in the world, I stand up and squeeze myself between his back and the lounge chair, placing my legs on either side of him. He tries to fight me, but I wrap my arms around his chest and pull him into me until his head settles below mine. My chin rests on the top of his skull, and I inhale the scent of him as I hold him as tight as I can in this moment.

We say nothing. We do nothing.

His shaking subsides after a few minutes, and he wraps his hands around my forearms, trailing his fingers through the hair there. "Sorry," he whispers.

"Nope. We don't do that shit anymore."

"Apologize? I thought we were supposed to do that now."

"I mean, we don't apologize for having fucking feelings," I tell him. He hisses when I pinch his side in warning. "We're gonna be all mature and shit. It shouldn't be this hard to express ourselves. No more running off."

"Man," River says, sighing. He tosses his head back and looks up at the sky. "This whole fucking time I thought she loved me. I've been sticking it out, trying to figure a way out for her, but she fucking left me a long ass time ago. On purpose, Pierce!" He throws his hands out as he stands and paces around the pool.

"River, sit down."

"I don't wanna sit down, Pierce. I want to go back home and—"

"And what, River?" I shout. "What are you gonna do to your mom? Kill her? Hell, give her more drugs and hope she finally overdoses? That's dumb."

"I want to kill my dad at least, man. He was... is... an abusive shit. He's done this to us. I bet he was the one who told my mom to do it, too. Rapture? Yeah. She tried that shit because of him, I just know it!" He looks out at the woods behind Riley's house and just... screams. The loudest scream I've ever heard. Guttural. Pained.

Cleansing.

He screams obscenities.

He screams his pain.

His voice cracks, and he falls to his knees.

Instead of being alone like he wants, however, I'm right fucking there, ready to grab on and hold him. I cradle his head in my hand and rub his back with my other, not saying a fucking word as he combusts in front of me. Hell, a tear slips from my own eyes as I feel his pain as if it were my own.

Again we say nothing. Do nothing.

"Fuck, this is embarrassing," he mumbles against my shirt, which is now soaked through where his tears fell.

"Don't let it be," I tell him. "It's just me, man."

"You don't get it, Pierce," he says, pulling away and wiping his face with his own shirt. "It's not only you. You mean as much to me as she does. Fuck, Pierce. I love you as much as I love her."

"I love you too, Riv, you know this." I start to stand, but he grabs my hand and pulls me into him. I land in his lap, straddling him and looking down at him. His eyes gloss over with more tears, and I lose myself in them for a few seconds.

"You don't get it, Pierce," he whispers.

My heart threatens to give out right there on the edge of the pool.

"Don't get what?" I ask, but I already know what he's been trying to tell me.

"I love you. Like... actual love, man. My fucking heart wouldn't be the same without you here. You're one of my soulmates, Pierce."

My eyes flick between his, and I take a moment to think up a proper response before swallowing more of my pride. "I love you too, River."

His grin grows so wide it's almost impossible to think he's the same man that broke down minutes before. Then his lips descend on mine and I don't give a fuck about anything but how we feel together.

How we've always felt together.

I screwed us over a million times in the past. Keeping him an arm's length away while I held out for Raven. I didn't realize until now how much he's been the glue that's kept me in one piece, and has cemented himself firmly between me and her.

I groan into the kiss, then pull back with my hands on his shoulders, grinning when I see how flushed his face is. "Not the time for all this shit, Riv."

"It's perfect timing. At least my dick says so." He wags his brows and I stand up with a dramatic sigh, holding my hand out for him.

"Come on. Let's go make sure Riley hasn't killed Nix yet."

"What makes you so sure Nix hasn't killed Riley?"

"With how tired he's been over Lexi dying?" I shake my head as I keep hold of River's hand. "Nix would go down fast and easy."

We walk back into the house to find Raven and the other girl sitting on the floor next to the coffee table across from one another. They share smiles, and apparently some fucking cookies, as they converse on a notepad.

When she sees us, Raven stands and rushes toward us, throwing her arms around River as tightly as she can. He releases my hand so he can hold her up and kiss her forehead. He takes a moment to breathe her in, no doubt calming himself further.

I smile at them both and stick my hands in my pockets as they have their moment.

"I'm all good, sweet girl. I promise," River tells her before placing her back on her feet. "Where's Nixy boy?"

Downstairs, she signs.

River meets my wide eyes with his, and we both rush toward the door Raven points at.

"I swear he's going to be dead. I can sense it." River rushes down the stairs and I follow with my heart thundering in my chest.

I'm going to have a heart attack before I'm thirty at this point.

"So long as you measure that out right, and keep the proportions exact, it will work." Riley is leaning against a solid stone countertop, his arms folded over his white coat, eyes narrowed through his safety glasses and his hands wrapped in blue latex gloves.

Phoenix looks much the same as he leans over a pile of paperwork. He pulls back and grabs a vial of liquid, then pours it into a larger one.

I'm not smart enough for this shit, so I keep walking into the room until I'm standing a safe distance away. "You're gonna help us out, Mark?" I ask. "Just like that?"

"He has conditions," Phoenix says. "Tell them, Mark." He nods his head toward us before getting back to the paperwork.

The man swallows harshly before he stands to his full height as if he's readying himself for battle.

And maybe he is.

"I want my daughter out of here. I want to rejoin civilization." He looks to the side and back at me.

"And?" I ask.

"I want Maxwell Langston to die." He nods his head once and squares his shoulders, watching me closely.

"Why don't you want your daughter to stay with you?" I fold my arms over my chest and lean against the wall.

"She's lived in this house for her entire life. She's smart, but only book smart. She needs street smarts. She'll need a social worker—"

"Hold on there," River says with a laugh. "We aren't going to take care of your daughter for you. How old is she?"

"Nineteen," he says. "You guys help get her on her feet, and I'll come back with you to manufacture enough of this anti-drug to dose the entire population of Cobalt City."

Phoenix looks up from his work, eyes wide in surprise. "He could find and kill you, Riley."

I glare at Nix. "The man's offering to help fix his own wrong, and you're trying to warn him away?"

He shrugs and looks back at Riley, waiting for the man to answer.

Riley sighs and his shoulders deflate. "Help my Beatrice, and I'll assist you until he finds me. If I survive, Phoenix said you boys have someone who can help me restart life. I'll do that away from my daughter, to keep her as safe as possible."

River laughs, staring at all of us like we're crazy. "I'm sorry, man. You think we're the safe place to be? We're dealing with a drug slash human trafficking scheme... and you want her to hang out around us?"

"Does the girl up there know how to defend herself?" Riley asks.

"Hell yes, she does," River replies.

Riley nods and says nothing more, turning his gaze to meet mine.

I look at Phoenix, wait for him to nod, then do the same with River. When he nods, albeit a little reluctantly going by the look of irritation on his face, I meet Riley's gaze, extend my hand and nod once. "You've got a deal."

I WON'T SAY I'm one to understand all the science bullshit going on in this basement, but I'm definitely intrigued by the recent developments... ones I hadn't had in mind.

"If we place this just right in the buildings, it'll blow everything in it and above it to dust." Riley grins as he sits back up on his stool, looking at Nix.

Nix, who's taken notes for the last six hours, poked and prodded and who knows what else with so many chemicals.

I knew I was holding his sorry ass back when I made him change his classes.

His brown eyes sparkle with excitement when he points to something and Riley nods excitedly. Nix folds his arms over his chest and looks over at us. "For the idiots in the room. We're making bombs. Big buildings on campus go boom." He fans his hands out and wiggles his fingers, pulling a laugh from River and me.

"We can't just blow the whole ass campus up, Nix." I stuff my hands in my pockets and shake my head. "We gotta come up with a way to get them off campus, except for Maxwell."

"And Jimmy," River says.

"I have other plans for Jimmy fucking Perkins," I grit out, and he nods as a wide grin stretches his lips. "That motherfucker deserves to have his dick cut off and fed to fucking pigs or some shit."

"We aren't murderers, Pierce," Nix says. He frowns when I meet his gaze. "We aren't. We may fuck people up and do a bunch of shady ass shit, but we haven't flat out murdered a soul before."

"I'm not so old that I can't learn new tricks, Nixy boy," River says.

Nix looks down at the paperwork with a sigh. His brow furrows as he looks over the notes. "We'll call Starling. He can help us."

I nod and stand up, yawning and stretching out my limbs. I've been on that stool for who knows how long, only standing to eat and use the bathroom. Watching Nix and Riley go over all of this has been boring as fuck, but I still don't trust the older man and I refuse to leave one of mine alone like that. "Where can we sleep?" I ask, looking at Riley.

"I'll come up with you and show you the guest rooms."

He stands and walks toward the stairs, Nix close on his heels, still asking questions.

We walk into the living room the girls are in, and they both look up from the books in their hands. I meet Rae's sheepish gaze and roll my eyes at her playfully.

"We only need one room, Mark," Phoenix tells him. He walks over and reaches his hand out for Raven, pulling her to a stand before wrapping his arms around her.

"Oh," Riley says. "Well," he clears his throat and nods. "Beatrice, would you show them to the second master suite, please?"

"Yes," she replies in a small voice.

I don't think any of us understand what's going on here, because one minute she seems scared of him and the next she's obeying him or wanting his safety. But that's a problem for another day since I guess she's coming with us now.

Whoever said doing good deeds made you feel better about yourself never took into account the exhaustion you get if you spread yourself too thin.

We follow them up the stairs and down a long hallway, where Beatrice opens an old ornate door to a large master suite. The bed might be a little snug tonight, but as Raven lays down on it and lets out a slow, exhausted sigh, I realize in that moment that I don't care who's squished. We all need the comfort.

Beatrice and her father leave, closing the door behind them, and the room falls silent as we all strip down to our underwear. Raven steals Nix's shirt to sleep in, then grins at all of us as we maneuver ourselves around her.

"I love you, Blue," I whisper in her ear. I kiss her softly

before laying my head down on the pillow between her and River.

Should be strange, this feeling of completeness I get between them, like they're calming every nerve ending with their love for me, but I've realized through this trip that I deserve it.

So... about Adeline...

RAERAE

You didn't tell me about her when you told
me about your dad abusing you in the
church, River. You kept her out of it entirely.
Why the hell would she allow a young child
to be abused like that?

I wasn't always a young child when he did
it, though.

RAERAE

You know that's entirely beside the point,
River. Don't fuck with me right now. I'm so
mad and on top of it I'm terrified because I
don't like the feeling of being followed at
all. Changing cars is scaring me. And then
we'll be out in the fucking open at the
amusement park and it's just... none of this
is okay.

I'm sorry. We're doing everything we can to
protect you. I promise. Plus, we have
Lance and his crew watching over us,
RaeRae. We'll be fine. I just know it.

RAERAE

Lance and his crew will have to sleep
eventually. You realize that right? Also,
don't say we'll be fine. You DON'T know it.

OK.

raven

Whoever said climbing out of a bed with three men was easy was lying.

I should know.

I've been debating if it'd be easier to slide down to the end of the mattress, climb over River and Pierce, or make my way over the top of Phoenix.

It's hot. I need to pee. And I'm surrounded by guys who are on such high alert I'm sure they'd pull out a knife if I sneezed.

Pierce groans and rolls over, burying his face in River's chest, and I smile at the sight, wishing my phone was closer so I could snag a picture.

There's a soft knock at the door and I give in, deciding to slide all the way to the bottom of the mattress, then stand as quickly as possible to not risk disturbing the guys. Hopefully, they won't think I ran off. I use the bathroom and wash my hands. On my way out, I pull my jeans on from yesterday, keeping Phoenix's shirt. He can claim it back later. When I open the door, I come face to face with Beatrice. She stands there in a bright yellow sundress, chewing on her nails as she waits for me.

Her lips curve into a sweet smile. "Raven," she whispers excitedly. "Will you come downstairs with me? I thought... well, we could make breakfast for everyone?"

I glance back at the boys, watch as their chests rise and fall with their deep breathing, then turn back to Beatrice and nod.

She grabs my hand as I close the door, then tugs me after her. Her movements are quick and quiet, and she keeps looking back at me. It's almost as if my presence is the best thing she's ever had in her life.

And maybe it is.

When I was talking to her yesterday through the notepad method she came up with, she confessed how she'd always wanted a sister or a best friend. She feels so lonely, but she knows she shouldn't leave her dad because she's all he's got now. Her mom died when she was four to a—surprise–drug overdose. My heart hurt for her as she asked me questions about the outside world. Like it wasn't right outside the gates of her father's estate.

It will be a challenge when we take her back with us, and after listening to the boys' concerns over dinner last night, I told them we wouldn't make her feel out of place. She may be our age, but she's been locked away for so long. I take it as a personal goal to help her acclimate before we let her go. If she wants to stay with us forever, she can, and the boys can shut up about it.

I grin when we step into the large kitchen, knowing Phoenix would have just as much fun in here as he did with the chemicals in the basement yesterday. He loves to watch how things react with each other. People. Food. Chemicals. Powders.

Hopefully, it won't take too long for them to get the anti-drug made, and we can take our own doses before he tries to scale it for the town.

"So," Beatrice says from outside of the cupboard. "My dad usually makes the pancakes, but I wondered if maybe you knew how?" She peers around the door.

I nod, and her smile grows.

"Perfect!" She grabs a package of pre-made mix, and I scrunch my nose up before walking past her.

I grab the sugar, flour, baking powder, and salt, and set them down before opening the fridge door. I grab milk, butter, and an egg, then put those on the counter.

If there's one thing Phoenix has taught me in the last few months, it's how to make everything I love from scratch, because it always tastes better that way. Somehow. I don't understand it, but it's magic, and he's never wrong about it.

Beatrice grabs a notepad and pen, then places it in front of me. "Why are you grabbing all of that, Raven?"

It always tastes better from scratch. You know it's clean and fresh. When you cook something for someone from scratch, they know you put all your love into it.

I shrug after she reads the note, then put things together. I toss a bit of vanilla extract and cinnamon in the mix, all while writing the ingredients and process down for Beatrice to follow.

It takes a while to cook pancakes for six adults, especially when three of them eat like hungry wolves. By the time I plate the last pancake, Mark sits at the table with a cup of coffee, and the thundering footsteps of my guys echoes in the hallway.

River makes it to my side first, leaning in for a quick kiss before heading straight for the coffee machine.

Pierce pulls me into a hug and kisses me until Phoenix clears his throat and shoves him aside.

Phoenix wraps his arms around my middle and presses sweet kisses to the back of my neck. "You made them with cinnamon," he says. It's a statement, not a question, but I nod anyway. "I love you, Red, and I'm so sorry for being absent."

I spin and wrap my hands in his hair, earning a glare for messing up the bun on his head. Our eyes meet, and he leans in for a sweet kiss. My heart thunders in my ears, and my smile hurts from how wide it is.

I love you, I mouth.

"I love you, too." He kisses my nose and turns to get his own coffee while I turn back to make sure everything is off before joining everyone at the table.

Breakfast is almost surreal, as if we're still on vacation and not here to fix my father's fuck-ups. As I stare around at my men, getting light touches here and there from each of them, Beatrice watches us all with a curious expression.

She devours her last pancake, sips from her orange juice, then clasps her hands together as she leans over the table. "Is this how everyone is? In most of the books I've read, it's always one guy and one girl. How does everything work? Who takes over responsibilities for certain things? Are you all *together* together or are you just with her?"

"Beatrice," Mark chokes on his last bite. He shakes his

head and wipes his mouth. "That's incredibly invasive and rude."

"She's fine," Phoenix says, an amused smile on his lips. He finishes his coffee and places his hand on my knee under the table, squeezing lightly. He meets my eyes, then looks over to Beatrice. "Honestly, Pierce was her first love, then he screwed everything up—"

"Hey!" the man in question shouts, glaring at Phoenix.

"Raven showed up at college on a phony scholarship, and the moment we all knew we wanted her, we set our egos aside and decided we could share her."

"What they're doing isn't typical by any means," Mark says, as if trying to dissuade his daughter from this relationship dynamic.

"It's hella convenient, though," River says through a mouth full of food.

"How is it convenient?" Beatrice says, brows furrowed.

"Well, we have less chores and stuff to do around the house because there's more of us. If someone is sick, it's easy to pick up slack because there's more of us. Not to mention the way we all get to—" River grunts. "Ouch!" He glares at Pierce, who shakes his head.

"Okay," Mark says, interrupting the rest of the conversation with a panicked look on his face. "Let's change subjects."

"But—" Beatrice starts, but Mark holds his hand up and shakes his head.

He looks over at Phoenix. "Before we finish this up today, I want to make sure you're being serious about taking Beatrice with you. You said you had an extra car to take us back up to Oregon with you?"

Phoenix nods and looks at Pierce. "Bring Lance in so

they can meet him really quick. River and I will work on cleaning this mess up."

River sighs, winks at Beatrice when she giggles, then stands and helps clean off the table.

A few minutes later, Lance enters the house, looking put together in his black slacks, white button-down, and suit jacket.

Why do you always insist on dressing so proper? I sign.

He laughs and signs as he talks. "It's part of the job description from Sam. Can't break the rules." He shrugs, then looks around the room. "Who am I meet—" He pauses when his eyes land on Beatrice. She stands next to the table with her arms wrapped around herself as she stares at him. Their eyes meet, and he clears his throat. "Who am I meeting?"

"Mark Riley," Pierce gestures toward him. "Riley, this is one of our security members, Lance. He's head of security right now."

Mark assesses Lance, eyes roaming over him from head to toe and back again before he squares his shoulders and extends his hand. "What's your last name, Lance?"

Lance straightens his jacket and extends his hand, gripping Mark's hand firmly. "Miller, sir."

"Can I trust you? You'll be driving me back toward a man who wants to kill me. Can I trust you not to drop me and my daughter at his feet?"

Lance nods once and exhales when Mark releases his hand.

"Lance heads up a pretty large team, and they've been on our backs this whole trip. Never felt safer, Riley," Pierce says, patting Lance on the back as he passes him.

Mark nods and relaxes, then turns toward Beatrice, who

is practically trembling with her nerves and blushing a bright shade of red. "You stay up here with Raven for the day, okay? We should be done by dinner. Get a start on packing your things up. We'll be leaving as soon as possible."

Beatrice chews on her lip, keeping her eyes plastered on the floor until her father walks down the basement stairs. She looks up and meets Lance's gaze again as she shifts around uncomfortably.

With a shake of my head and a smile, I turn away from them to see all of my guys standing in the kitchen. They cross their arms over their chests as they stare at me, and I clench my thighs together on instinct. They look like predators, and I hope like hell I'm their prey.

Phoenix nods his head toward the stairs, and I turn around, walking up them without question. "We'll be down after a shower, Riley," he calls before he follows me.

I barely make it inside the door before they descend on my clothes like they're offending them.

River removes my pants, Pierce follows him with my underwear, and Phoenix claims his shirt back before collaring my throat and grinning at me. A threat in his gaze.

"I really did mean the shower," he says, backing me toward the en suite.

Pierce and River slide their hands over my naked body before they head into the bathroom. The shower starts a moment later, and my breathing picks up.

"We've neglected you the last two days, Red. Hell," he breathes. "I've neglected you for this entire trip, and I hate it. I'm sorry."

I shake my head, but when I go to raise my hands to sign, he clutches both of my wrists in his and puts them behind my back. He cuffs them in one hand and returns the other to my throat, still backing me into the bathroom.

Pierce comes up behind me and kisses my shoulder while he slides his hands down my sides and over my ass. "It's going to be a long, long day without you, little bird."

"We want to make sure you don't need us at all, but also that you don't forget us, little vixen." River leans toward me, and Phoenix turns my head so we can kiss.

The steam from the shower fills the room as quickly as the arousal floods my veins. When Pierce reaches down and slides a finger through my folds, I buck against his hand, and Phoenix groans.

All at once, they back away from me and remove their clothing. Phoenix lifts me in his arms and brings me under the hot water, and I hiss between my teeth when it sluices down my back.

"Too hot for you, Red?" he asks.

I shake my head and bring my arms up to wrap around his neck. He groans when I scratch his skin, only to push me up against the tiles of the shower and thrust into me in one smooth movement. He steals my breath as he stares into my eyes, claiming my body and soul all at once. It only lasts a few minutes before he finishes inside of me with a long groan, stilling himself as his breathing returns to normal. It's a quick, dirty, yet passionate fuck, leaving me wanting more. Unsatisfied. Yearning.

He passes me over to River after kissing me, then cleans himself off.

I gape at him, wondering what the fuck their plan is. Are they really passing me around like this? Am I... liking it?

River chuckles in my ear as he moves, carrying me to the showerhead again just as Pierce slides up behind me. The water cascades down my back, and when River repositions my legs around his hips, spreading me open, my eyes widen and I look down.

"You aren't even close to ready for that yet, little vixen," River says. He leans in to kiss each of my nipples.

Pierce lifts his hand, already lubed up, and shoves a finger inside of me. I toss my head back onto his shoulder as he works me over, River's mouth still teasing my chest.

"You see," River says in a hauntingly dark tone. "Nixy boy has a lot of work to do, and while he'd love to be the one fucking you until you see stars, he just doesn't have the time. So Pierce and I took the hard task on for ourselves. Didn't we, pup?"

"Yes, we did," Pierce says, kissing my shoulder before resting his chin on it and meeting River's gaze.

"I'm gonna let that slide, because we're running out of time," River says, his tone a warning. "Be a good pup and stick your dick in our girl's ass, will you? Her cunt is dripping all over my dick right now."

"Yes... master," Pierce grits out.

I wonder if they'd ever record a private session between them for me to watch, so I can see this submissive side of Pierce in all his glory.

"Whatcha thinkin' about there, little vixen?" River asks with a raised brow.

Biting my lip, I shake my head and wrap one arm around Pierce's neck just as he shoves inside of me. My mouth pops open as he settles and River thrusts into me without warning. I lock my ankles behind his back and try to move my hips, but they keep me pinned with their hands.

River nods, Pierce groans, and they fuck me ruthlessly in unison. I'm never not full of one of them, and sometimes I'm full of both. It's a flurry of sensation, and with the extra gravity, I fall onto them over and over.

Pierce moves his hand to collar my throat as his other pins my hip in place. He whispers in my ear. "You're the glue that holds this whole fucking crew together. You know that?"

I nod, and he squeezes my throat tighter.

"I fucking love you, Raven Marie Hill. Till death do us fucking part, you got that?"

My heart stops beating, and I stop breathing in that moment as my eyes shut and I clench around them both.

"We're all at your feet, Blue."

River leans forward and claims my mouth with his as they find their rhythm again. He shoves a hand between our bodies and massages my clit, and within seconds, I detonate around them. I feel my cum coat River's dick and lower stomach, and he groans just as Pierce does. They lose their rhythm as they chase their release, until they smash me between them, plastering kisses on me and groaning sweet nothings against my skin.

It's erotic, passionate, and empowering.

River pulls away first, looking dumbstruck as he gazes into my eyes. I smile for him as he slides out and goes to clean himself off, clearing his throat. A faraway expression takes over his face that I'm not sure how to fix for him.

"He'll be fine," Pierce whispers in my ear. He soothes my worry and my aching skin, then helps me clean off before tending to himself.

As we step out of the shower, he meets my eyes in the mirror and grins that boyish grin I fell in love with, and I spin around to hug him extra tight in my arms.

The greatest gift I could have ever asked for is having my best friend back.

"TRIS," Beatrice says aloud suddenly.

We're in the living room, packing up the last of the things she wishes to bring.

Hint: Books. Always more books.

I glance over at her and tilt my head to the side in question.

"I want to be called Tris. Not Beatrice." She nods her head as if confirming her own decision. "Beatrice makes me sound too old and too fancy. I'm none of those things."

I shrug as I put the last book in the cloth bag she brought down and fold my arms over my chest.

"Will you teach me how to sign, Rae?" she asks. This is about the tenth time today she's asked this, and she squeals again when I nod.

I don't mind spending time with her, but the combination of adrenaline and exhaustion is getting to me, so her constant excitement is only draining me more. Not her fault, totally mine. Still draining, though.

"Does it ever stop raining in Oregon?" she asks.

I sit down on the couch and nod, trying to hold back my laughter.

"If I want to go to college, are you guys going to help me sign up? I mean, I'm enrolled online but I don't want to be online anymore and—"

"River!" Pierce shouts just before their footsteps pound up the stairs. "River. Do not run out like that, man."

River ignores him as he rushes out of the front door, slamming it hard enough a picture falls off of the wall.

I flinch when it breaks, and rush over to Pierce before he can leave, too. I place a hand on his chest and shake my head as I meet his gaze.

"Blue, I can't just leave him out there by himself. I don't want him to suffer alone. I—"

I lean up on my tiptoes and kiss him softly before I take a step toward the door. *I'll help him this time. You go help in the basement*, I sign.

He opens and closes his mouth, struggling to come up with an argument, then sighs and nods his head once before walking away.

The moment I step out of the house, I hear River shout, and take off running.

river

"Mom?" *I sit on the ground and grab the bottom of her dress. I pull it so many times, but she doesn't answer me. Or move at all.*

I'm getting scared.

She keeps staring at the TV, but it's not even playing the cartoons she told me she'd put on.

"Mommy?" I cry, but wipe my tears away because Daddy wouldn't like that I was crying. He says God didn't sacrifice his son for us to cry over silly things.

Everything is a silly thing to Daddy. Except God and Mommy and me. So I listen. He's older, and sometimes meaner. Says one day I'll be just like him. I want to be like him because he has lots of friends who give him lots of money at church every Sunday. Daddy says money helps keep us fed and happy, so I gotta make money like he does.

But right now Mommy isn't answering me, and I'm getting really really scared. I take a deep breath and put my hands together and start praying. Cause God fixes everything.

That's what Daddy says.

"Please God. Please help Mommy hear me. I don't know why she's not hearing me, God. Are her ears not working? Make her ears work again! Perform a miracle like you did in your big book!"

"Get off your knees and come finish dinner, River." Daddy walks into the room and leans over Mommy, hiding her from me. He says something so quiet I can't hear, and a tear falls down her pretty face.

"What's wrong with Mommy?" I ask him in my big boy voice. He'd be mad if I whined. Can't whine. Can't cry.

"Don't worry about your mother, River. I said go finish dinner." Daddy snaps his fingers and points to the kitchen, and I know when he snaps he's real mad, so I listen and go where he tells me.

There's a bunch of stuff ready for spaghetti to be made, so I do what Mommy taught me and get it all ready. I burn my hand on the pot when I pour the water out, but I don't cry. Can't cry. Not allowed.

My step stool breaks when I try to climb up and get plates, so I have to grab another chair and pull it over. I try not to make noise, I really do, but Daddy comes rushing in.

He grabs me by the arm and yanks me out of the way, snapping his fingers and pointing toward the corner.

I don't say anything as I go where he tells me.

Standing in the corner, I push up on my toes and put my nose on the sticky note held high enough I have to stretch my neck.

As Daddy finishes dinner, all the dishes make lots of noise and so does he when he starts yelling about having to do everything for everyone.

I make a promise to myself and God in that moment: when I

start third grade tomorrow, I will be the best helper ever, so he won't ever be mad at me again. And maybe Mommy will be able to hear me, too.

FUCK. Fuck. Fuck!

I thread my fingers through my hair and pull hard, trying to get the pain to manifest physically.

It doesn't. It never fucking does.

"Fuck!" I shout as loud as I can toward the trees. For as long as I'm yelling, the world silences and nothing in my brain works. But I can't scream forever, and have to stop when my voice cracks. "Fuck," I whisper.

I wipe my face with the bottom of my shirt, then jump when arms wrap around me. I spin and am about to shove whoever it is off of me, but then I see her and, for some stupid fucking reason, I crack. Again.

I'm so tired of cracking in front of people. I'm not supposed to.

Or I wasn't supposed to.

It's hard to re-parent yourself.

I bundle Raven in my arms and plaster my face into her shoulder as I sob, shaking with the brutality of my emotions. I don't know how else to handle this but to hold her while she holds me. My heart is breaking and I don't know what the fuck to do about any of it. I feel like I'm the one dying and everyone around me gets to live.

When do I get to live?

"I'm... I'm sorry, Rae," I whisper into her skin, now wet

from crying. I pull back and use the top of her shirt to dry them off with, then look down into her eyes, misted over by her own tears. Guilt wraps around my gut and I take a deep breath, trying to center myself.

She places her hands on either side of my face and yanks me down until my forehead rests against hers. Then she takes a deep breath.

I watch as a tear falls down her cheek. Reaching up, I catch it with my thumb before wrapping my arms around her again, pulling her into me. "I'm so, so sorry."

She shakes her head and pulls back enough so she can sign what she wants to say. *Having emotions isn't something you should ever apologize for. Not ever. Not around me or the guys. We are your safe space, River.*

Although it should feel like a bunch of bullshit and pretty words, my heart aches for the feeling they all provide for me. The love, the caring, the honesty. All things I never truly had.

I kiss her once, then pull away and walk us over to the lounge chairs where Pierce and I sat yesterday.

God, was it yesterday? Feels longer than that.

I sit down in the chair, and Raven climbs onto my lap, straddling me but keeping her distance so she can talk to me. I place a hand on her cheek and brush my thumb over her skin as I watch too many emotions flicker over her face. "You're so fucking beautiful, Rae," I whisper.

She smacks my hand away and glares when I laugh in response. *What happened?*

And while I know she means just now to cause me to come outside like that, I can't help but think of the first time I learned about my mom's issues. "At first," I begin. "My dad would tell me my mom was sick. She had some rare disease or whatever bullshit he could come up with that week. But as I got older, they started having drug talks in school and told us what could happen. I think it was around fifth or sixth grade that I made the connection to my mom." I take a deep breath and close my eyes because the look on Raven's sweet face pains me. "I confronted my dad about it, and he said she needed the medicine she was on because it kept her alive. For two years after that, I believed him. Then I started high school, and someone pointed out how my mom looked like she was always high. I got into a fight over it. Physical fight. Beat the guy up real good and got suspended." I open my eyes and watch Rae's expression as I tell her the next bit. "My dad told me that night that my mom did all the drugs because she couldn't put up with me. That I was always too much. Too loud. Too energetic. Too chaotic."

That's so fucked, Rae signs.

I shrug. "After that, I got real quiet. Kept doing what he said, and hoped like hell Mom would stop doing so many drugs. At that point, his excuse was that she'd been on them so long she'd never be able to get off them. Of course, it was my fault, so I only had myself to blame." I laugh and shake my head. "That's kind of where my head's been at since. I got into CU, and I think it was him that convinced them to let me in. My grades sucked in high school."

They don't know, she signs.

"Nope. I want to get away from him. Really get away. So I said I'd use my brain for good and get a good degree, good job, and leave. Course, until now, I had planned to take Mom with me." I swallow, but when a tear falls and I go to wipe it away, Rae takes it away herself, keeping those pretty blues locked on me.

Why don't you have the same plan now? Rae signs.

"They're all making a plan for what to do to take revenge. It's all turned to some major conspiracy and we're going to call in the original crew. See if they'll apologize, or if they care. Whoever we deem worthy... they get to leave, I guess. I said I'd happily get my dad there, but not my mom. I don't want to betray her." I huff out a laugh and turn my head to stare out at the trees. "That's when Pierce reminded me she used to leave me with shitty babysitters so she could go party and get high."

Rae shifts uncomfortably, and I reach forward, grabbing her and turning her until her back is to my chest, and she sits between my legs. She slides her fingers between mine and rests them on her stomach and we just... chill.

I don't relax often, but lately it's always been with her. She breathes new life into me and allows me to be me. I let a smile stretch my lips as I lean down to kiss her head and breathe her in. "Hey, you remember the top of that coaster?"

She tenses in my arms but nods.

"Turn around a sec."

She sits up, turns around, and crosses her legs before meeting my gaze.

I place my hands on her cheeks and break into a smile for this moment, because she deserves it. And so do I. "I was gonna tell you I love you, Raven. Like really love you. You've clawed at the scarred organ in my chest and made it bleed for you. I'd say only you, but Pierce has it, too." I grab her hand and place it over my chest, smiling when a tear falls. A happy tear. "This? This is yours and his. I mean, Nixy has some of it too, I guess, but that's not the same. This is the forever kind of love, sweet girl. I just needed to tell you that."

The smile that breaks free on her face feels as if the sun is shining down on me after a long, dark winter. I laugh when she launches herself at me, wrapping her arms and legs around me like a little koala.

"Does that mean you love me, too?" I ask.

She pulls back and signs, *I do love you. So much. So, so much.* Tears fall from her eyes and this time I don't wipe them away, and neither does she. She presses her lips to mine and threads her fingers through my hair, pulling me impossibly close to her.

I place my hands on her hips and hold her against me, not wanting to let her go for a millisecond. This kiss is a remnant of the one we shared in Pierce's room during the pineapple prank.

No.

This kiss is the roaring fire created from the sparks of that night. Our hearts barely looked at each other back then, and now here we are, about to take revenge and finally start living life. Together.

Whether that's for a few months, or a few lifetimes, I don't know.

What I *do* know, however, is that Raven was the breath of fresh air we all needed this year, and I can't wait for our crew to finally soar.

"WHERE THE HELL have you two been?" Pierce yells at us as we reenter the house. He pulls Raven into his arms and hugs her tightly before putting his hands on her shoulders and looking her over.

"Afraid I hurt her?" I ask, raising a brow at him as I cross my arms over my chest.

"You guys were gone for two hours!" He lets Raven go and rushes toward me. Instead of hitting me like I think he's going to, he wraps his arms around me in a tight hug, breathing me in for a few seconds. He pulls back and looks me over, then does the same to Raven before shaking his head. "I don't know what I thought. My gut's all fucked up right now."

Is something wrong? Raven signs.

"Not right now, no. I just... something feels off."

"About Riley?" I ask.

He shakes his head. "Let's just... get down there. There are a few more steps and some other shit to take care of before we'll have the anti-drug." He looks at Raven as she walks over to sit beside Beatrice on the couch. They're already pouring over a new book when he calls out, "Hey Blue?"

She looks back at him with a soft smile and tilts her head in question.

"I love you."

She grins wide and mouths the words back while signing them.

Beatrice looks at us all and places her hand over her chest. "You guys are so sweet! I love it!"

I chuckle. "Love you too, RaeRae," I call out as I follow Pierce back down the basement stairs.

"Ah, the final love confession," Pierce says, laughing when I shove his shoulder. "You okay?"

I shrug and walk further into the basement. "We'll get them both. But if my mom, for some reason, actually apologizes or seems sympathetic..."

"We'll get her out before the bombs go off," Phoenix says. "Got it."

I nod once and exhale when Pierce wraps his hand around mine. Looking over at him, I feel the support I've always had, but now I know I deserve it.

RIV

Hey, RaeRae?

Yeah?

RIV

I love you.

I love you, too, River.

RIV

Okay. So now that's out of the way…

What do you want?

RIV

Well, while we're down here making these drugs… which… hold on a second.

picture of Phoenix dressed in a lab coat and safety goggles

Why does that turn me on? Damn.

RIV

Sometimes I wish he'd get in on the action with me and Pierce because I would ABSOLUTELY fuck him. You're lucky.

Anyway. We know it's gonna be weird having Beatrice live with us. We were wondering if you had any idea on where she should stay?

We can use the old shed. Make it into a tiny home for her or something.

RIV

That's fucking perfect! The guys said we'll get on it as soon as we get back home.

Oh, and RaeRae?

Yeah?

RIV

Can't wait to get home and show you how
much I love you.

raven

I don't remember the last time I had a friend that wasn't Pierce, so sitting here for the past few hours with Tris has been a complete and utter whirlwind on my emotions.

I've been teaching her basic sign language phrases, and she's already picked up on a lot in a short time period. She's insanely smart, which is going to help when we show her the world outside of this estate.

Thank you, she signs, then squeals in excitement.

Okay, so the squealing needs to stop, but I don't want to rain on her dopamine parade, so I smile along with her.

"That should do it," Mark says as he ascends the stairs. When he comes around the corner, he looks at Tris and smiles. "Ah, Beatrice!"

"Tris," she corrects him. When he tilts his head in question, she sighs. "I want you to call me Tris now. Beatrice sounds too formal."

Mark looks like he's about to have an aneurysm, but he

smiles tightly and nods. "Okay then, Tris. How was your day?"

"It was good. Great!" She tells him about our afternoon, and I tune her out in favor of watching my boys enter the room.

Pierce and River each kiss my cheek as they pass by to sit on the other couch. I grin when they lean against each other. I've never been prouder than when I watch them get comfortable with their sexuality. Well, Pierce at least. River would probably be comfortable if a pineapple found him sexually appealing.

I cover my mouth to hide my huff of laughter and shake my head.

"Alright," Phoenix calls as he enters the room. He stops at the end of the coffee table and places down a small box. When he lifts the lid, I lean forward to see what's inside.

I knew they were working on the anti-drug today, but I expected it to be more...

Just more.

There, in four simple clear vials, is a yellow liquid. There are needles set off to the side, and Phoenix pulls out some antibacterial wipes. He holds them out to the other two before using one on himself, and I sit back, raising my brow.

"Red," he sighs.

I hold up my hand and stand up. *You don't expect me to take one?* I sign. *What are you worried about? Clearly nothing if you're planning to put that shit in your veins.* I fold my arms over my chest and clench my fists, holding back more nasty words and accusations. They wouldn't help this argument, anyway.

Phoenix's jaw tightens, and he shakes his head as he

leans down to hand the vials to the other two. All three of them fill their syringes before sharing a meaningful look. Phoenix looks back at me and his eyes fill with an emotion I can't quite decipher through my haze of anger. "If we're doing good in the morning, you take your dose. But until then!" he shouts, as I lean forward to grab the last vial.

I pause and peer up at him, angry tears now blurring my vision.

"Until then, Red, please trust us. Okay?" He swallows and looks down at the needle and back at me. "We'd die for you. All we ask is that you don't die with us."

I briefly run my finger over the last vial as I watch the three loves of my life shove needles into their skin with a drug manufactured in the house like we're qualified for this shit. They wince and hiss, as if it burns them, and my gut screams at me to tell them to take it out. Take it back.

We could run away, right? Ignore Maxwell. Go to a different country...

But the people in Cobalt City would suffer...

Countless others would suffer...

We may be dumb college kids, but this was our chosen path, and we need to be on the right side of history when it comes to this.

But damn if those boys think I'm going to sit back and let them be stupid without me.

"HEY RAERAE," River calls from the other side of the guest room door.

255

I came up here over three hours ago. It's midnight, and it's achingly obvious they're doing just fine now. Not a single one of them has come up to give me my intended dose.

"Just... we'll see you in the morning, okay? I... love you." He taps the door a few times, and I watch his shadow retreat.

"RED," Phoenix calls thirty minutes later. "I know you're still awake."

I roll my eyes. If he expects me to open the door right now, he's delusional. I'm pissed the fuck off, and I only locked myself away for their safety.

A thud sounds from the other side. "You realize you snore, right? These soft little snores that shouldn't be as cute as they are." He chuckles. "If you don't want to sleep with us tonight, that's fine. Just know that I love those and I'm going to miss them tonight."

I want to tell him he's the one to talk when it comes to snoring, but I refuse to open the door, so I wrap the blanket around myself and turn onto my side, watching the shadows formed by the trees outside.

"I love you," he says, and I listen as his footsteps retreat.

THE SOUND of a knock on the door and the rattling of the doorknob wake me up.

"You're being incredibly stubborn tonight, Blue," Pierce says. There's a rough thud and the sound of shifting fabric.

I turn to watch as his shadow consumes the bottom of the doorway as if he's sitting against it.

As silently as I can manage, I walk over to the door and sit against it as well. I can hear his breathing from the other side and it calms me, even if I am mad as hell. I lean my head back against the wood just as his finger slides under the door. Grinning like a fool, I move my hand until our fingers lock, and he lets out a long sigh.

"We fucked up, Rae. I know that, but we're not sorry for it. I love you. So fucking much." He tightens his hold and I sigh. "Nix said it best, baby. We'd die for you, but we don't want you dying for us."

I pull my finger from his and turn around, kicking the wood once to get my point across as I storm back toward the bed and slide under the blanket.

After I've taken my dose, those boys can incur the wrath of blue balls until they apologize for their bullshit.

Asshats.

I YAWN as I make my way down the stairs. It's around three in the morning, and I'm unbearably tired.

I heard the boys as they shuffled off to bed. They're only a few doors down from the guest room I holed up in, so I gave them about half an hour before I made my escape.

Not really an escape, more like... a middle-of-the-night adventure to go take an anti-drug none of us know works.

As I turn the corner, I jump about a mile in the air when I

see Tris sitting on the windowsill, wide awake as she stares out of the window.

Directly at Lance's car.

At first she doesn't see me, and I'm able to grab the supplies I need. But as I try to make my way out of the room, she calls my name and I whip my head around.

"I hope you know how much they love you, Raven. I only wish someone will love me like that one day." She shrugs and looks back out of the window. "Either they're being stupid, or you are. None of my business, though."

I walk into the downstairs bathroom, closing and locking the door as quietly as I can. When the harsh light blinds me, I wince and close my eyes until the dots stop surfacing. I pull my sleeve up to expose my veins and pump my fist until they're clear. I clean the area, fill the syringe, take a deep fucking breath because motherfucking hell I hate needles and plunge it into my arm.

Fire instantly burns through me and I take a seat on the toilet lid, tossing my head back as tears threaten to fall. It only lasts a minute, but fuck, it leaves an impression.

I toss everything into the trash and step out into the hallway. Worrying that the guys might catch me at the top of the stairs, I walk out of the back door and sit on one of the lounge chairs, allowing my body to relax and come down from the adrenaline and frustration of the night. The night air cools my skin, and the stars are so pretty out here. No fog. No city lights to compete with.

An owl hoots in the distance, and I laugh at myself when I flinch. But then a twig snaps, and I rise to my feet.

Is someone fucking out here?

Did River come back out here?

Maybe it's just Lance patrolling the grounds. Making sure we're safe.

I nod to myself and walk back toward the house, wanting to step inside and feel safe again as my heart hammers in my chest and my breathing becomes erratic.

The gate creaks open at the side, and my palms grow sweaty as I try to open the back door. It's hard to turn a doorknob when your fucking hands are slick, so I dry them off on my pants before I try the door again.

Footsteps sound on the pavement.

The door still won't fucking budge.

I bolt.

I take off like a bat out of hell, away from the footsteps and around to the other side of the house. Halfway toward the front, a twig snaps, and I turn around to see someone in a hoodie right on my fucking heels.

I wish I could scream and yell at this moment, but I can't. I fucking can't because I lost my fucking voice a year and a half ago and now I'm this panicked fucking woman running from a predator in the night.

Tears fall down my face as I continue toward the front lawn. Just as I go to round the corner, however, my head is covered with a cloth bag.

I thrash, twist, kick, bite, spit, to no fucking avail.

My assailant grabs my wrists and ties something plastic around them. Zip ties?

They chuckle, and the sound of it halts my movements. Ice floods my body as fast as shock overcomes me.

"Well, hey there, sugar."

You know what's coming...

TO BE CO....MPLETED IN THE FOURTH AND FINAL NOVEL OF A CONSPIRACY OF RAVENS. COMING IN JUNE 2023!

acknowledgments

This book was different. So much so that I questioned the entire thing.

While writing it, I had the flu (twice), covid (once), the stomach bug, and who knows what the hell else that decided to try and take me out.

My family went through some major life changes, and we had to learn to grieve something that isn't a death.

But through it all... I still managed to finish the damn thing.

And learned something in the process: take a moment to appreciate the small moments. They matter most.

So, dear reader, please know that those moments that make you smile in the middle of the day? Those are the moments we should strive to enjoy the most, because they're far more frequent than the big successes we all chase at the end of the day.

I want to thank my little family for helping me through this and helping me plot the entire road trip for this book! I hope we get to take the same route one day, just for fun.

To Drea and Kendall... you girls are my goddamn rocks. Thank you. I love you.

Kennady... never leave me. You know too much.

Brandi, Tori, Jennifer... you can't leave me either. You're

all so invaluable to me. Thank you for the tough love, and for convincing me this book is as amazing as I wanted it to be.

To my Ream subscribers... you guys make it possible for me to continue on this journey. Thank you for your ongoing support.

And to my readers... thank you. I hope you had fun reading this and aren't too mad about this cliffy.

Book 4 is coming soon, and then we'll be on to a whole new journey with some new & old characters.

Sincerely,

Shelby Lee